"*I want you, Arizona!*"

"There's a saying about hell and fury and women scorned—are you sure you're not suffering from being scorned, Declan?" she asked scathingly.

He laughed. "It could be a bit of that, too, I guess."

"On the other hand, what would you have thought of me if I had responded to your eyes across the fence?"

"Well, I probably wouldn't have had to marry you, would I?" he said placidly.

LINDSAY ARMSTRONG was born in South Africa, but now lives in Australia with her New Zealand-born husband and their five children. They have lived in nearly every state of Australia and have tried their hand at some unusual, for them, occupations, such as farming and horse training—all grist to the mill for a writer! Lindsay started writing romances when their youngest child began school and she was left feeling at a loose end. She is still doing it and loving it.

Books by Lindsay Armstrong

HARLEQUIN PRESENTS
1656—UNWILLING MISTRESS
1713—AN UNSUITABLE WIFE
1770—A MASTERFUL MAN
1798—TRIAL BY MARRIAGE
1874—DANGEROUS DECEIVER

LINDSAY ARMSTRONG

Married for Real

Harlequin Books

TORONTO • NEW YORK • LONDON
AMSTERDAM • PARIS • SYDNEY • HAMBURG
STOCKHOLM • ATHENS • TOKYO • MILAN
MADRID • WARSAW • BUDAPEST • AUCKLAND

ISBN 0-373-11925-9

MARRIED FOR REAL

First North American Publication 1997.

Copyright © 1996 by Lindsay Armstrong.

Printed in U.S.A.

CHAPTER ONE

ARIZONA Adams flung her large black hat on a settee, crossed the lounge to the mirror over the fireplace and withdrew the pins securing her thick hair. She ran her fingers through it as it fell to her shoulders in a rich river of chestnut. It was strong, abundant hair with a bit of a wave in it, and she could do pretty much as she liked with it. Her late husband, who had died a year ago and whose memorial service she'd just attended, had often commented that it had a life of its own.

She sighed and looked at her elegant outfit, an almost ankle-length slim black dress worn with a long cream jacket, and thought he would probably have approved of it. He'd also often said that she had an innate but different sense of style, although he'd been fond of adding that she could wear anything and look good. But the truth was, she did her own thing when it came to clothes, and for some reason it generally came out right—then again, according to her mother, she always did her own thing pretty much, which was fairly ironic coming from her mother, who had named her only daughter after a song first and a state in the USA quite incidentally. Yet here she was, Arizona reflected also with irony, feeling tense and uneasy as well as sad and not at all sure whether she would be allowed to continue to do her own thing.

She turned away from the fireplace and glanced at her watch. Nearly six o'clock, which left six more hours of this day—would he come?

He came five minutes later.

Arizona heard the doorbell chime just after she'd shed her jacket and was picking up her hat. She stilled, and right on cue the double lounge doors opened and Cloris stood there.

'Sorry, Arizona,' she said diffidently, 'I know you didn't want to be disturbed but it's Mr. Holmes. I—well, I didn't like to say no.'

'That's all right, Cloris,' Arizona said resignedly, laying her hat and jacket down with exaggerated care. 'I'm sure Mr. Holmes is a hard man to say no to.'

Cloris, who liked to think she enjoyed a more exalted station than housekeeper but who nevertheless was a marvellous housekeeper, smiled gratefully. 'He was at the service,' she confided. 'At the back—I don't think many people saw him. I only saw him because I was at the back myself and, well—' she gestured '—that's Mr. Holmes.'

'That's Mr. Holmes,' Arizona echoed. 'Show him in, please, Cloris.'

Cloris beamed then hesitated. 'Would you like me to bring in some, er, drinks and snacks?'

'No,' Arizona said definitely.

Cloris opened her mouth but detected the gleam in Arizona's grey eyes, and she withdrew with a suddenly shuttered expression. Arizona grimaced. Ten seconds later Declan Holmes walked into the room. He was, as Arizona had often heard commented, a fine figure of a man. Tall and well built, he had thick dark hair and Irish blue eyes. That he often had a saturnine, cynical look in those blue eyes didn't seem to lower him in the estimation of many women by an iota. If anything, it was the opposite. Which was a fact that she'd thought about once or twice with some cynicism herself—her own sex's preference for dark, damning men. And, as she'd often seen him, he was faultlessly outfitted in a dark grey suit that hid neither his powerful shoulders nor lean hips and justly became his position of wealth and power.

'Hello, Declan,' she said coolly and with some idea of taking the initiative as he stopped a few feet from her. 'So you did come.'

He raised a wry eyebrow at her. 'I don't break my word lightly, Arizona. How are you? I believe I'm to be denied the pleasure of having a drink with you.'

She narrowed her eyes and said a bare, 'Yes.'

'That's a bit harsh, isn't it?' he murmured amusedly. 'You look as if you could do with one yourself. It can't have been an easy afternoon.'

'And about to become even harder, I imagine.'

'We'll see,' he said placidly. 'Did you really think I wouldn't come? I thought you knew me better than that, Arizona.'

'It's strange you should say that, Declan, because I hardly know you at all,' she retorted.

'Now that, my dear, is not quite true,' he replied. 'I think it's fair to say we've been—eyeing each other over the fence for a couple of years now.'

A flash of anger lit her eyes. 'I have not been eyeing you or anyone else over any fence,' she said precisely.

He moved his shoulders slightly. 'Well, put it this way— I've certainly been eyeing you, Arizona. And I'm equally certain that you have not been unaware of it.'

She tensed inwardly and would have loved to be able to deny this with composure and surety. Unfortunately, although he'd made no overt moves at all, she had been aware, by some inner sense, of Declan Holmes's interest. There had been times right from the day they'd first met when she'd looked across a room and encountered his blue gaze, times, she couldn't deny to herself, when something within had responded, some curl of interest had awoken—which she'd thoroughly despised herself for. And correspondingly there had been times when she'd gone out of her way to avoid him, only to be visited by the uncomfortable feeling that he'd known exactly what she was doing and why... *But I'm damned if I'm actually going to admit anything to him.*

She said matter of factly, 'A lot of men look.'

He smiled a little dryly. 'One of the hazards of being such a good sort, I guess.'

Arizona shrugged. 'I don't really care whether you think I'm vain, Declan.'

'As a matter of fact I don't—just honest, in this case. Do they all ask you to marry them?' he enquired guilelessly.

Arizona was saved having to reply as there was a knock at the door. It was Cloris, looking pink and determined, which didn't happen often, but when it did she was as tenacious as a miniature bulldog with faded blonde curls. She had with her a trolley with an array of drinks and a plate of snacks, and she stood in the doorway staring beseechingly at her boss. Arizona closed her eyes then said in a goaded sort of voice, 'Bring it in, Cloris, bring it in.'

And so Cloris spent a few fluttering minutes deploying her trolley and departed finally in an even worse flutter after a few kind words from Declan Holmes.

Who said to Arizona once the door was closed again, 'Routed, I'm afraid, Arizona—are you going to take it in good grace? In other words, may I pour you a drink and myself one and may we then sit down and discuss—things more comfortably?' But there was a gleam of mockery in his blue eyes.

Arizona breathed deeply, shrugged and sat down. 'Thanks, a brandy and dry,' she said briefly.

He poured two of the same, handed her hers then sat down opposite her. 'Cheers. Well, here's to the fact that I'm here to ask you to marry me as I promised I would twelve months ago—to the day,' he said gently, sipped his drink then placed it beside him.

'And you haven't, in the intervening twelve months, reflected that if nothing else it was pure bad taste to ask me that on the day of my husband's funeral?' she retorted.

'On the contrary, I think advising you of my intentions but allowing a whole year to pass before I acted on them was observing all the proprieties. Particularly in view of the fact that your last marriage was a marriage of convenience, Arizona.'

'How dare you?' She stared at him coldly.

'Let's examine the facts then,' he replied smoothly, 'and don't forget I knew Pete well. But you came here to Scawfell as a penniless governess, didn't you, Arizona? To look after the four motherless children of a man twice your age. Less than a year later you married him, and all this—' he gestured, taking in the elegant room and somehow more, the whole beautiful estate of Scawfell '—became yours.'

'No, it didn't,' Arizona contradicted through lips pale with anger. 'It's held in trust for his children, as you very well know, Declan. After all, you're the trustee.'

'All the same, you have the use of it guaranteed until you remarry, Arizona,' he said coolly, 'and the means so that you can continue to use it in the manner to which you've become accustomed.' His eyes lingered on the smooth skin of her bare arms then drifted down the exquisitely tailored black dress.

'I didn't want that, I didn't know it was in his will,' she said steadily. 'Nor have I done anything in the manner to which I had become accustomed, quote unquote, since Pete died, other than look after his children and—'

'How are they?' he broke in.

'Fine,' Arizona said briskly. 'Why don't you ask them how I rate as a stepmother, incidentally?'

'I've never accused you of not being a good step-mother, Arizona,' he returned mildly.

'Only a fortune huntress,' she said with soft mockery.

'Well, why did you do it?' he countered.

'Marry Pete?' she said with hauteur. 'That's my business, Declan, and I'm afraid you're destined to remain in ignorance.'

'Even when you're married to me?'

She took this without a blink and said thoughtfully, 'Tell me something—considering what good friends you were, didn't you think it was in incredibly bad taste to be eyeing your friend's wife across the fence, as you put it yourself, Declan, if *nothing* else?'

'Unfortunately one can't help one's—instinctive reactions. And as I did nothing but look on the odd occasion, no, I don't.'

'And what would have happened if Pete hadn't died?' she asked caustically.

He shrugged wryly. 'Who knows? I might have got tired of looking, although I'm not sure about that. Or you might have got tired of Pete.' He grimaced.

Arizona ignored this and said, 'But, and this does puzzle me, you now want to marry me, despite the fact that you think I only married Pete with an eye to the main chance. That doesn't altogether make sense, if you'll forgive me.'

'I think it makes perfect sense,' he responded. 'I have a much larger fortune than Peter ever had, which makes me an excellent candidate for your hand—provided, of course, you reserve that lovely, sexy—' he looked her up and down '—body for my exclusive use,' he finished, looking into her eyes with a gleam of pure insolence in his.

'That's incredbly—that's diabolical,' Arizona said with an effort, an effort to stay calm. 'You're talking about trade, nothing else—'

'I rather thought you understood about trade all too well, Arizona,' he broke in.

'Contrary to what you think, Declan, I was extremely fond of Pete,' she said, and stood up restlessly.

'But you weren't in love with him?' he said after a moment as he sat with his arm along the back of the settee and watched her thoughtfully.

'I...' She stopped then looked directly into his blue eyes. 'It wasn't a grand passion, *if* they exist.' She shrugged. 'But yes, I loved him in a way. A warm,

committed way that I can't imagine ever loving you.'
And her grey eyes were suddenly challenging.

'Would it surprise you to find yourself loving me
in a different way?'

'Are you talking about love or lust?' she asked with
an insolent glint of her own.

'They're not always easy to separate, Arizona,' he
drawled.

'Oh, I think they would be in this case.'

A faint smile twisted his lips, then he sat forward,
picked up his drink and regarded its depths for a
moment before he said, 'Well, my dear, this may be
the moment to talk turkey then. Pete's rather complicated estate has finally cleared probate, and unfortunately, the outlook is not good at all.'

Arizona frowned at him. 'What do you mean?'

'You may not have realized this, but Scawfell is
heavily mortgaged and was, to an extent, mortgaged
against Peter's future income, which should have
payed it off—he was one of the most famous, sought-
after architects in the country. What he neglected to
do, however, was take out any insurance against, well,
the unknown happening such as did happen.'

Arizona sat down rather suddenly. 'What are you
saying?'

'I'm saying,' he said levelly, 'that although he was
the finest architect, he wasn't much of a businessman.
He was also very secretive so that not even I knew
how complicated his affairs were or how unwise some
of his investments. What it boils down to is that
Scawfell will have to be sold to save anything of his
estate for his children, let alone the provisions he made
for you, but in the real estate climate of the moment,

it's debatable if there will be anything left for any of you.'

'But I don't understand,' Arizona whispered, paling as his words sank in. 'He never said a word to me about all this, not—' she stopped then continued '—not that I ever asked him. But he didn't seem to have any worries about finances.'

'He wouldn't have had if he hadn't died so unexpectedly.'

'But...' She stood up again, uncaring that he was watching her like a hawk now. 'This is terrible! It was bad enough for them to lose their father like that, in a car accident, after losing their mother to an incurable disease and with no living relatives—'

'Which was why as their trustee I agreed to them staying with you, Arizona,' he said with a significant little look. 'They don't have anyone else, no grandparents left alive, aunts or uncles et cetera because both their parents were single children.'

'I *know* that. And to lose Scawfell as well,' she said hollowly. 'Are you sure?'

'I'm sorry to have to say I'm all too sure.'

'So...what will we do?' She stared at him dazedly. 'Ben is enough of a handful at the moment as it is.' She stopped abruptly and bit her lip.

'So they're not all fine—what about the others?'

Arizona closed her eyes briefly then said a little bitterly, 'I'm sure fifteen-year-old boys can be a handful without the trauma he's gone through—'

'Oh, I'm sure they can,' Declan Holmes replied dryly. 'Especially without a father. What about ten-year-old twins—and Daisy?'

'How did you find them on the last of your monthly visits?' Arizona countered.

He looked amused. 'My monthly visits that you so pointedly went out of your way to avoid whenever you could? Daisy was—Daisy,' he said. 'The twins were extremely taken up with the model I brought down, and Ben was out, too.'

Arizona sighed. 'Sarah and Richard do seem to have bounced back, but then they have each other,' she said of Peter Adams's ten-year-old twins. 'As for Daisy, it took her months to understand he was never coming back, then she got weepy for a while, but I think she's forgetting now, although she tends to cling, but I'm always here so—Ben is the only real problem.'

'How so?'

'He's moody, he seems to have given up on school— he seems to hate the whole world, other than his horse and riding, at times.'

'I see.'

'That's a great help,' Arizona remarked after a pause.

'I didn't think you wanted my help.'

'I don't, but you insisted on knowing. Look,' she said impatiently, 'this is getting us nowhere. How come no-one has seen fit to let me know about all this before today?'

'A lot of it wasn't known for a time. There were offshore ventures that took quite some time and patience to unravel.'

'But I don't understand,' she said, perplexed. 'How have we been going along in the meantime?'

Declan Holmes paused, narrowed his eyes and said, 'I hope you don't hate this too much, Arizona, but with my help.'

She gasped. 'Do you mean you've been support- ing us?'

'Precisely.'

'But why didn't you tell me?'

He said reflectively, 'I had several motives, Arizona. I didn't want to add any more burdens for the kids to have to cope with so soon after losing their second parent, and I thought it would be difficult for you to carry on unconcernedly once you knew.'

'Well, you're right,' she said through her teeth, 'but it would have been on their behalf not mine that I would have been unable to remain unconcerned despite what I have no doubt you're implying!'

'Perhaps,' he said mildly.

'So what were your other motives?' she demanded.

He raised an eyebrow. 'I guess I wanted to see how you did—conduct yourself over the last twelve months.'

'Before you came back and asked me to marry you again? How do you know I haven't taken a legion of lovers in the interim?'

'Have you?'

Arizona made a sound of pure, despairing exasperation.

'Look, don't answer—I know you haven't,' he said with a lightening grin.

Arizona opened her mouth, closed it then all but spat, 'Have you been having me followed or something like that?'

'No, nothing like that, but I do have my sources,' he replied imperturbably. 'In fact,' he continued softly, 'it's almost as if you've been waiting for me, my dear.'

'So...it's never entered your calculations,' she said with difficulty, 'that I might just have been grieving and not interested in forming any liaisons?'

'Well, one day I'll probably know a lot more about you, but in the meantime, will you marry me, Arizona?'

'No. Definitely not,' she added to give it more force and then tried a little more force. 'It would be the very last thing I'd do. Do I make myself clear?'

His blue gaze didn't alter much—perhaps a tinge of amusement crept into it. 'Not even if I told you that it was one way, probably the only way, to save Scawfell for Pete's kids?'

Arizona realized suddenly that she could hear her heart beating heavily, that her lips were dry and her breathing ragged. And nearly a minute passed before she said in a voice quite unlike her own, 'What do you mean?'

'I mean that if you married me I would pay off the mortgage on the estate so that the children had something to inherit as well as a familiar beloved spot to live out their childhood, and I would support them as my own—as our own.'

'Do you mean you would bring them up as your children?' she said uncertainly.

'We could bring them up as ours.'

Arizona stared at him dazedly then licked her lips. 'What's the alternative—for them, I mean?'

'Well, I would certainly never let Pete's children starve, but taking them on single-handedly wouldn't be the same for them— I'd probably have to relocate them. I wouldn't have a great deal of time for them although I suppose I could always get another governess for them.'

'Stop,' she whispered then cleared her throat. 'This is the most arrant blackmail I've ever heard—*why?*' she asked intensely.

'Why?' he mused. 'I should have thought that was obvious—I want you, Arizona!'

'There's a saying about hell and fury and women scorned—are you sure you're not suffering from being scorned, Declan?' she asked scathingly.

He laughed. 'It could be a bit of that, too, I guess.'

'On the other hand what would you have thought of me if I had responded to your eyes across the fence?'

'Well, I probably wouldn't have had to marry you, would I?' he said placidly.

'That doesn't make sense—it's worse,' she declared bitterly. 'It puts me in a no-win situation, which is simply crazy!'

'Well, now, that remains to be seen. Being married to me won't be nearly so bad as you're cracking it up, Arizona. At one stroke you'll retain Scawfell, you'll retain four children you're very fond of and who need you—think of that if nothing else.'

Arizona closed her eyes and for the life of her couldn't help thinking of it. Thinking of Daisy, whose natural mother had died when she was two, Daisy who didn't remember her and didn't understand about stepmothers and thought Arizona *was* her mother, Daisy who worried... Thought about Sarah and Richard, charming twins so long as you understood the full extent of their dependence on each other, and Ben. Poor, tortured Ben who was still bereft without his father, who now viewed the world with cynicism and disenchantment and was increasingly disruptive... She opened her eyes and stared blankly at Declan Holmes.

'Also,' he said quietly, 'you'll have your sex life taken care of—and an awful lot of pin money to spend, Arizona.'

'If I didn't hate you before, I do now,' she responded equally quietly.

He smiled briefly. 'But you'll do it?'

'Only because I have no choice.'

'Not entirely true,' he drawled, 'but nevertheless, when?'

'Oh, I think I'll leave it to you to name the day, Declan.'

'Is that some kind of a cop-out, Arizona?' he murmured.

'No,' she said baldly. 'Merely an indication of my lack of interest.'

His lips twisted but he said only, 'How about a month from today then? It will give the kids a bit of time to get used to the idea.'

'If you say so—me, as well, I suppose.' She grimaced.

'You've had a lot longer than that,' he remarked softly. 'If it's so repugnant I'm surprised you haven't left the country or something equally dramatic.'

'But you knew damn well you had me here as some kind of a hostage, didn't you, Declan?'

'Did I?' he reflected. '*Exactly* what *kind* of a hostage, is what one wonders, to be honest. While I don't doubt your devotion to the kids—oh, well—' he gestured with one long, strong hand '—time will no doubt tell. Why don't you invite me for the weekend, Arizona? We could start the process of apprising the world of our intentions.'

'Come, by all means,' Arizona replied with utterly false cordiality. In fact her stance and the look in her eyes said something quite different—come and do your damnedest, in other words.

To which, after a long, challenging moment, he merely smiled gently as if to say, *We'll see, we'll see...*

'Dearest Mother,' Arizona wrote that night. 'I suppose it's still all right to call you that and not Sister Margaret Mary, but I digress. The news is that I'm getting married again—now I know how you opposed, from the seclusion of your convent, my first marriage but from a purely materialistic sense, this one is even better. You've probably heard of Declan Holmes—who hasn't? Yes, the same one who took over his father's media empire (small media empire) at the age of twenty-six and now, at about thirty-three, could probably be justifiably termed a media magnate. Well, he was a good friend of Peter's, he's the children's trustee and guardian and as I'm the children's stepmother, it seems like a good idea. So far as your objections to my previous marriage go, he's only ten years older than me, he's not a father figure or anything like that, he's a mighty marriageable man, but no, I'm not in love with him and I don't think he's in love with me. What else can I tell you? It's to be a month from today...'

Arizona lifted her head and stared into the middle distance. *Can I tell you that I'm incredibly confused, desperate and afraid? That I'm wondering whether I should leave the country or something like that—but how to leave the kids?*

She closed her eyes then impatiently tore the sheet off her notepad and threw it into the wastepaper basket. A moment later she reached down and tore it up into little pieces, which she let fall like confetti into the basket, thinking at the same time that it was a cheap shot writing to her mother like that, that it was continuing a feud that should be over, that if the one thing her mother had done right in her life, it seemed she was making a good nun.

The next morning as she dressed, she observed the slight shadows under her eyes, grimaced then tossed her head. She pulled on jeans and a blue sweater, tied her hair back and went on her rounds of waking the children. And when they were dressed and assembled at the big table in the kitchen, she went out of her way to be as normal as possible over breakfast, served by Cloris.

'Let's see, Sarah and Richard, you have drama this afternoon after school. Daisy, you're going to play with Chloe straight from school and I'll pick you up at five o'clock and Ben—'

'I know exactly what I've got on, thanks, Arizona, you don't have to treat me as a child,' Ben interrupted intensely.

'Okay!' Arizona smiled at him and got up to give Cloris a hand with the school lunches. 'Oh, by the way,' she said casually over her shoulder, 'Declan is coming to spend this weekend with us.'

'Yippee!' the twins chorused, and Daisy followed with a similar exclamation.

It was Ben who said moodily, 'What's he coming for? I thought he was here yesterday.'

Arizona narrowed her eyes. 'And I thought you liked Declan, Ben.'

'He's all right,' he said ungraciously. 'But what is he coming for?'

'It doesn't matter what he's coming for, Ben,' Daisy said earnestly. 'What matters is that he's nice and we should be nice back, shouldn't we?'

'For God's sake,' Ben entreated, 'can't you make her stop lecturing us, Arizona? She's only six—'

'Ben—'

'And you shouldn't say that,' Daisy continued solemnly. 'Should he, Arizona? I mean talk about God like that?'

'Eat your breakfast, Daisy,' Arizona said smoothly.

'But I'm right, aren't I?'

'Yes, you're right,' Arizona replied with the patience of long practice.

'Well, for crying out loud then,' Ben muttered moodily, 'what happened to the old saying about children—' he glared at his baby sister '—being seen and not heard?'

'Daisy not heard!' Sarah said with a giggle.

Richard piped up, 'That'll be the day!'

Whereupon Ben got up and flung out of the kitchen with his breakfast half eaten.

Cloris wrung her hands and murmured something about growing boys, Daisy embarked upon the hazards of not eating one's meals and wasting away, Sarah and Richard became convulsed with giggles, and Arizona raised her eyes heavenwards as she wondered where this golden, solemn little girl had inherited her lecturing and worrying tendencies from—because

Daisy worried dreadfully about everything and never hesitated to expound upon it.

'It's all right, pet,' she said to Daisy. And later when she dropped Daisy off, last, at school, reassured her once again.

'Ben's not really cross with me is he, Arizona?' Daisy hung back in the car.

'No, but it might be an idea not to, well, lecture Ben at the moment.'

'What's lecture mean?'

'Uh—tell him what he's doing wrong all the time—'

'Because he might go away and never come back? You wouldn't ever go away and never come back like Daddy did, would you, Arizona?' Two large tears began to glisten on Daisy's lashes.

'No, no,' Arizona said hastily and gave her a quick hug and a kiss. 'Look, sweetheart, there's Chloe waiting for you. Now, don't forget you're going home with Chloe and her mum after school!'

When she got back to Scawfell it was to find Cloris in a suppressed state of excitement. 'Staying for the whole weekend, Arizona?' She beamed widely. 'I've already started on the blue bedroom and I've made a little list of menus—what do you think?' She fluttered a piece of paper at Arizona.

'I have absolute faith in you, Cloris, just don't make it too grand.'

Cloris managed at the same time to look pleased yet slightly crestfallen. 'Well, all right,' she said slowly then smote her cheek. 'The garden,' she said anxiously. 'It's in a bit of a mess and we've only got two days, it's Thursday today—'

'I'm about to attack it, Cloris,' Arizona reassured her.

'Well, you are so good at it, but I did wonder if we shouldn't get a gardening firm in, and then there's Ben!' she added dramatically. 'What do you think is wrong with the poor boy?'

Arizona looked at her ruefully. 'Still missing his father I would say—Cloris, don't get into too much of a flutter about Declan Holmes, he's only a man.'

'I know.' Cloris blushed nevertheless. 'But it is a bit of an honour to know him, don't you think, Arizona?'

'As a matter of fact I don't.' *Oh, hell,* Arizona thought immediately, *I'm going to have to do a bit of an about-face soon, aren't I?* And with an impatient grimace, took herself off to attack the garden.

She backed the ride-on mower out of the shed and started on the wide expanse of lawn in front of the house. Scawfell, which Peter Adams had inherited from his parents, was situated on the south coast of New South Wales and comprised about fifty acres. The house was old, two-storied, large and rambling on the outside, but over the years Peter had redesigned the inside so that it was light, modern and very comfortable. It stood with its back to a tree-lined ridge and faced, over its several acres of lawn, the sea. There was a fairly steep cliff face beyond the lawn down to a perfect little bay with a crescent of sandy beach. It was a wonderful place to live if you liked the outdoors, sweeping vistas and the sea. Arizona, born in a city and carted from city to city, excepting while

she'd been training to be a teacher, had taken to
Scawfell and country life as if she'd been born to it.
Always an energetic person, she'd found she loved
gardening, grew her own herbs and vegetables and
had reclaimed the orchard from a charming wil-
derness to a garden of bounty. She'd also had the
stables renovated, and at present they housed three
hacks and three ponies. All of which Declan Holmes
had been paying for, she thought with a sudden pang.

Which led her to think further, as she drove the
mower expertly and the scent of freshly cut grass filled
the air, that she'd been proud of her achievements in
her three years at Scawfell, proud in her first year as
governess of what she'd achieved with Pete's children,
then in her second year all she'd achieved with his
estate. *And I even thought I was holding it all together
over this last year,* she reflected a little bitterly. *Little
to know... at least I was a model of thrift and re-
sourcefulness. Little to know that the money Declan
was feeding into the bank as per the arrangement after
the will was read and until probate was his own. Not
that it's helped me much, being so thrifty and re-
sourceful, he still views me with the utmost cynicism
and he's still determined to marry me...*

She sighed again and thought of Peter Adams, who
had been a vague, warm, friendly man, a genius at
designing buildings but not a good businessman, apparently, yet a man who had understood her and had
known something of the forces that had moulded her.
Why did he have to die? she thought sadly. *For the
first time in my life I felt... safe.*

She spent that day and the next working extremely
hard, often alongside Cloris although certainly not in

the same mood. But she couldn't deny that she was also motivated to have Scawfell looking its best. It was unfortunate that Declan Holmes, who'd said he would arrive on Saturday morning, arrived late on Friday afternoon, catching her unkempt after a bout in the orchard. But the news he brought with him upset her all the more...

CHAPTER TWO

SHE was crossing the driveway, hauling the dead bough of a peach tree, when he drove up in his dark red convertible Saab.

She dropped the bough and stood with her hands on her hips as he stopped the car only feet from her. It was a windy, cool dusk with the promise of rain in the air, and she wore a pair of denim dungarees over an ancient checked shirt, wellingtons, gardening gloves and had her hair bundled into a red scarf.

On the other hand, as he opened the door and stepped out of the Saab, she saw that he was wearing well-pressed khaki trousers, highly polished brown moccasins and a white knit sports shirt beneath a beautiful dark brown leather jacket.

'What are you doing here *today*?' she said crisply as his blue eyes drifted amusedly over her.

'Came a bit early, that's all,' he drawled. 'Is there a problem?'

'You could have warned us!'

'Sorry,' he said entirely unrepentantly. 'But if you're embarrassed about how you look, may I say that it makes no difference what you wear, you still look like a goddess, Arizona. Although in this case an avenging goddess,' he added with soft mockery.

Arizona's expression defied description for a moment, then she said tautly, 'Cloris will be thrown into despair. She'd planned to roll out the red carpet for you and make every meal a masterpiece, whereas it could well be mince on toast tonight.'

He laughed. 'I quite like mince on toast, and I loathe red carpets, but I will make my formal apologies to Cloris.'

'Not to me, though.' She gazed at him coolly.

'I really don't think there's anything I need to apologize to you for, Arizona, is there?' He raised an eyebrow at her.

'No, nothing!' she marvelled. 'Well, if you'll excuse me, I'll get rid of this and—'

'Incidentally,' he broke in as she turned away, 'I'll be staying for the week.'

She turned back immediately. 'A *week*! Why?'

'I felt like a break, that's all.' He shrugged. 'And seeing as we're betrothed, who better to spend it with than you? Of course I didn't expect the prospect to fill you with *undiluted* joy, but—'

Arizona muttered something under her breath and went to turn away again, whereupon he stopped her with a hand on her wrist. 'But we do have a bargain, don't we, Arizona?'

'Let me go,' she said proudly.

'In a moment. Don't we, Arizona?' he repeated evenly.

'Yes,' she said through her teeth. 'However, in *private*, Declan, *don't* expect much joy at all!'

His blue eyes narrowed but he said merely, 'And in public, Arizona?'

'I have no idea how—things will come out,' she said through her teeth.

'Then you better start thinking about it,' he replied dryly. 'Or thinking about the kids,' he added with all the pointedness of an unerringly aimed arrow. 'Are they all home?'

'No. Ben is out camping with his scout group.' She paused then decided not to tell him that Ben had not intended to go on this camp—until he'd heard about Declan Holmes spending the weekend with them. So she added instead with a scornful toss of her head, 'I'm not in the habit of placing children in the line of fire, Declan.'

'Good,' he murmured. 'Then allow me.' And he picked up the bough. 'Where do you want it?'

Arizona gazed at him for a long moment but his eyes were a placid, mild blue. 'Over there, thanks,' she said briskly, pointing towards a pile of timber. 'I thought we might have a bonfire tomorrow night, if it doesn't rain.'

'Sounds like fun,' he said casually. 'Stay there, I'll drive you up to the house.'

'Won't you be bored stiff—here for a whole week?' she said abruptly as he drove the short distance to the front door.

'No. Why should I?'

'It's not exactly a dashing lifestyle we pursue,' she said with irony.

'It's not exactly a dashing lifestyle I'm after. And I thought it would be nice to—ride with you, swim with you, that sort of thing. We could also,' he went on as she cast him a weary look, 'go over the estate together and decide what needs to be done.'

'There's quite a lot—' She broke off and castigated herself mentally.

'Quite a lot to be done? Good—we're here, Arizona,' he murmured gravely, but his eyes were full of amusement.

'Well, would you mind if I left you to Cloris's tender mercies for a while, Declan?' she returned swiftly and sweetly. 'I rather desperately need a bath.'

'Not at all, Arizona, not at all.'

She took with her, upstairs to the privacy of her own suite, a raging tendency to want to swish her tail like an angry lioness.

Her suite, which Pete had designed specially for her, comprised a bedroom, bathroom and study. The bedroom faced the sea and was large and airy with a pale green carpet, an exquisite, riotous bedspread with the same green background and dusky pink and soft lemon tulips all over it, and draped green curtains. The study overlooked the rose garden she'd started at the side of the house, and each piece of furniture, the desk, the lovely winged armchair with matching footstool, the bookcase, were lovingly chosen antiques.

None of it, although it was usually a haven of peace and privacy for her, brought her any peace, however, as she strode into the peach marble bathroom, ran the taps and stalked to her walk-in wardrobe. And she rifled through her clothes impatiently before choosing a pair of slim cream pants and a taupe knit top.

In fact it wasn't until she was lying in the bath, surrounded by a sea of bubbles with her hair tied on top of her head, that she started to relax at all, and even then it was only in a limited sort of way. *How am I going to cope with him in front of the children?* she wondered despairingly. *If they haven't sensed my antipathy by now they must at least know we're not the best of friends.*

But although she soaked thoughtfully, then scrubbed and finally got out to dry herself on one of the outsize peach towels, no inspiration came to her. *Perhaps I can only follow his lead,* she mused dismally as she drew on her underwear and then her clothes and sat at the vanity table.

An *avenging goddess,* she thought bitterly as she studied her reflection. Damn the man! *But I can't go on thinking like that, can I? So what do I think about instead?* she asked herself dryly as she brushed her hair until it shone and left it loose to float in a chestnut cloud to her shoulders. *What it will be like to be married to him?*

She closed her eyes briefly then smoothed moisturizer onto her skin and made up her face lightly, just a touch of foundation, a light lipstick and shaped her eyebrows with a little brush, and answered herself, *No, I just can't picture it but then again, I can't picture how to extricate myself, either!*

She stood up suddenly and caught sight of herself in the full-length mirror on the opposite wall. She was five foot nine and knew that she had a willowy figure with some luscious curves that attracted men like bees to a honeypot. Her mother had had the same kind of figure.... To go with it, she had smooth skin like pale honey, luminous grey eyes with dark-tipped lashes, a well-defined mouth, and she could look thoughtful and serious, sometimes serene and happy, often impatient and autocratic but always, according to Peter Adams, amazingly good to look at.

She sighed and turned away abruptly.

What she found when she went downstairs was not exactly what she'd expected. The table was laid for dinner in the large, bright kitchen, which was normal. But it could have only taken Declan's charm to persuade Cloris to feed *him* in the kitchen. And he, the twins and Daisy were working on a model galleon in the rumpus room adjacent to the kitchen, separated by a half wall. Cloris was happily attending to a leg of lamb. It was a contented, domesticated scene. She paused just inside the doorway and thought of Ben, out camping in the windy darkness rather than being here, with a little sigh. But the only living thing that seemed to afford Ben any consolation these days was his horse, Daintry.

Declan Holmes looked up and saw her. 'Arizona—' he straightened '—you look . . . refreshed.'

'Thanks,' she said briefly, bit her lip then walked into the rumpus room. 'How's it going?'

'I think we're making progress.' He looked at the three absorbed, bent heads around him, and Arizona suddenly remembered that he'd brought the galleon for the children on his last visit.

'That was a good idea,' she murmured, gesturing. 'We keep it for that rather difficult hour to fill between bath time and dinner time.'

'Yes,' Daisy said earnestly. 'We're not allowed to touch it until we've had our baths.'

'That's why we've been so slow,' Richard said ruefully. 'We could have finished it weeks ago, couldn't we, Sarah?'

'Sure could.' Sarah didn't raise her head, so engrossed was she.

'But that wouldn't have been right,' Daisy began.

Whereupon both the twins raised their heads and said exasperatedly, 'Daisy, don't *start*.'

'I only mean—'

'Come and have a drink,' Arizona said wryly to Declan Holmes.

'With pleasure.' And when they were sitting in the lounge with their drinks, he said, 'How do you cope with her?'

'With patience and humour and just sometimes a desire to tear my hair out. Ben—' She stopped.

'Go on.'

'Ben,' she said after a moment, 'is finding it particularly hard to take at the moment, but then he's finding it all hard to take. I suppose—' she bent her head and paused in thought then shrugged. 'I don't know. But I'm worried about Ben. I can't get through to him.'

'I'll have a chat to him when he gets home.' He stretched his legs out and looked at her reflectively. 'In some respects you're amazingly mature, Arizona.'

'And in other respects?' she countered coolly.

'That wasn't meant as an insult.'

'Perhaps I'm so used to them from you I just expect them.'

'Or perhaps you're determined to turn everything I say into one. But before—' his lips twisted '—this degenerates into a slanging match, I meant that for someone of only twenty-three you're—capable. You run this place well, you look after the children well.'

'That still doesn't explain what you meant by in some respects.'

'At times,' he said slowly, 'your attitude to me is, well—' he shrugged '—quite naive. And sometimes, very rarely, you look young and untouched—but that's only when I catch you off guard.'

Arizona stared at him and felt an odd prickle beneath her skin. She was saved having to make a reply by Cloris announcing dinner.

* * *

'For a mince-on-toast type of dinner, that was excellent,' Declan murmured to her after they'd partaken of roast lamb with mint sauce, roast potatoes, pumpkin and sweet potato, baby green peas and rich gravy followed by an apple crumble and cream.

Her mouth curved into a fleeting smile. 'I would dearly have loved to serve you mince on toast tonight but of course I didn't reckon on Cloris.'

'Mince on toast!' Cloris said right on cue and in a scandalized manner. 'I only ever give you that for breakfast. What could you have been thinking of, Arizona?'

'Don't worry about it, Cloris,' Arizona murmured with a wry look. 'Just me being foolish, or is it naive? Okay, kids.' She stood up. 'One hour of television since it's Friday night and your favourite program is due to start in ten minutes, which will give you time to give Cloris a hand! And we could take our coffee into the office, Declan. There are a few things you might be interested to see.'

Declan Holmes stood up. 'Unfortunately I have a few calls to make, Arizona. May I use the office for those first? And your fax? We can have our little get-together when I'm finished.'

'By all means,' Arizona replied airily, although she was actually seething inside. 'I have a million things to do myself—in fact I have a better idea. Let's leave it until tomorrow!'

'Oh, no,' he said smoothly. 'Later this evening will do fine.' And he further infuriated her by helping Cloris and the children clear the table.

It was nine o'clock—she'd spun out the bedtime stories and rituals as long as she could, consoling herself that it was Friday night—before they came together again. And this time he was waiting for her in the lounge when she came downstairs, slightly dishevelled, after an energetic romp with the children before putting their lights out firmly.

'How about that coffee now, Arizona?' he drawled and indicated the trolley with a bubbling percolator that Cloris had left.

'Thank you, yes.' She walked over to the mirror above the fireplace and ran her fingers through her hair.

'All bedded down and correct?' he queried as he poured. She turned away from the mirror.

'Hopefully.'

'Lucky kids,' he commented and handed her a cup.

She sat down in her usual chair, wondered what to say but before she had a chance to wonder much, he said, 'There are a couple of things we ought to discuss, Arizona.' And sat down opposite her.

'I'm sure there are.' She shrugged. 'I don't feel much like it at the moment, though.'

'Well—' he paused and looked at her wryly '—perhaps that's what we should discuss first.'

'I don't know what you mean,' she murmured and smothered a yawn.

'I mean, taking the first step towards—putting you in the mood for everything we need to sort out.'

'I still don't know what you mean,' she said and stopped abruptly.

'My dear Arizona,' he said a little dryly, 'we're going to have to start somewhere and some time.'

'If you're talking about going to bed—'

'By no means,' he interrupted with an amused, mocking little look. 'Just getting to know each other a little better. I certainly wouldn't expect you to sleep with me without some sort of a—courtship beforehand.'

'Declan, if you expect me to indulge in some *petting* with you,' she said witheringly, 'you're wasting your time!'

'Don't you go in for that sort of thing? I don't blame you,' he said ruefully. 'It sounds awful.'

'Then what?' she demanded.

'We could try something a bit more sophisticated,' he suggested.

'Along the same lines but by a different name?' she said bitterly. 'No, thanks.'

'So you object to it by any name,' he murmured. 'Only with me?'

She stared at him and frowned. 'I don't think I get your drift.'

'I was just wondering whether you're at all awakened, Arizona. I've wondered it before, and then you did tell me that Pete wasn't a grand passion, if they exist, quote unquote,' he said gently, but it was a fairly lethal sort of gentleness.

Arizona reacted in several ways. She mentally bit her lip at the same time as she mentally took umbrage and finally came out fighting. 'Wouldn't that be a disaster,' she murmured with a faint smile. 'To think that you, Declan Holmes, who could probably have any woman he chose, took a frigid bride—dear me!'

'I didn't say frigid,' he replied after subjecting her to an insolently considering little scrutiny—from her head to her toes but particularly the curves in between. 'I said unawakened, which is an entirely different thing, Arizona.'

'Oh, I know!' she conceded with some mockery and added an insolence of her own. 'I also know how particularly prone men are to imagining they and they alone will be the one to do this... awakening.'

He narrowed his blue eyes thoughtfully. 'And that sounds as if you have cause to be particularly cynical on the subject, Arizona. Like to tell me why?'

'No—that is,' she amended after the first bleak negative sprang to her lips, 'you don't have to be a genius or particularly cynical to work it out. Men—' she waved a hand '—are men.'

'How entirely magnificently damning,' he said, but this time with genuine amusement.

'Not especially,' she said with a shrug. 'Just realistic.'

'Do you really believe that?'

'Why shouldn't I?'

'Was Pete like that?'

She looked at him straightly. 'I've told you before, Declan, that's none of your business.'

'And I disagreed with you, Arizona, but we won't pursue it at the moment—'

'You're going to find it hard to pursue at any moment,' she said impatiently and stood up. 'I think I'll go to bed, if you don't mind.'

'Yes, I do mind,' he said simply.

She looked at him incredulously. 'You don't imagine you can dictate what time I go to bed, surely?'

'Do you usually go to bed at this time?' he countered.

'No,' she said unwisely, 'but—'

'Then you're only being childish,' he said mildly. 'Sit down and finish your coffee.'

Sheer frustration caused her to sit down. 'I'm *not* a child—how dare you treat me like one?'

'All right.' He laid his head back and regarded her with a wicked glint in his eyes. 'Would you rather I said you were being tiresomely female?'

'No, I would not,' she replied shortly. 'Because, if anything, you're being tiresomely male. If you want me to stay we'll need to talk about something else.'

'Such as?'

'Scawfell, the kids, the weather—we have a huge range at our disposal.' She regarded him with a tinge of malice.

He laughed. 'Why don't we try something a bit more interesting. How you grew up and where, for example.'

'Wherever it was the whim of my mother to be at the time,' Arizona said briefly.

'What about your father?'

'I never knew him. He...deserted my mother upon discovering she was pregnant.'

'Ah,' Declan Holmes said.

'What does that mean?' she enquired tartly.

'Why you're anti-men—'

'I'm not. I would never have marrried one if that was the case.'

'Perhaps you married Pete for other reasons. Such as security, all this.' He overrode her as she opened her mouth. 'And perhaps,' he continued, 'it wasn't only the security of his supposed wealth you sought, Arizona, but protection from other men.'

Arizona set her teeth and gazed at him angrily. 'Such as you, Declan? You could be right.'

'Am I?' he murmured, unperturbed.

'That's something you'll have to work out for yourself,' she returned. 'I'm amazed the thought occurred to you,' she added candidly. 'I assumed you thought I was all bad.'

'Not at all. I've told you you're a good stepmother, a good manager et cetera.'

'You've also offered me, by way of marriage, the inducement of your wealth, Declan. If that's not the ultimate insult, I don't know what is.'

'You forget that I also offered you the means to keep together a family that means a lot to you. But principally, you're forgetting the kind of . . . pleasure we could bring to each other.' He looked at her blandly.

'Yes, well, I only have your word for that—it didn't take long to get back to that subject, did it? I am really going to bed now, Declan.' She stood up with an air of finality written all over her.

He laughed at her softly and wickedly but stood up. 'Very well, my dear. Good night.'

'Is that all?' Arizona said unguardedly and feeling as if she'd had the wind taken out of her sails.

'What more would you like?' he asked with a hatefully raised eyebrow. 'I thought you were dead set against any demonstrations of . . . affection.'

She turned away abruptly and with a slight flush staining her cheeks. 'I am.'

'Although we could always shake hands,' he murmured from right behind her. 'Would that be in keeping with your view of our relationship, Arizona? A purely business affair.'

'*Yes*,' she said through her teeth, swinging back. 'You've got *one* thing right at last, Declan.'

But he still looked only wickedly amused, and she was suddenly acutely conscious of his height and physique, the way his clothes sat on his well-built frame and how wide his shoulders looked beneath the white-knit sports shirt, how lean his torso and long his legs in his khaki trousers . . .

She realized suddenly and too late that she'd unwittingly fallen prey to that curl of interest Declan Holmes had been able, always able, she thought with a pang, to arouse in her, but not only that, make her hate herself for. *All right,* she thought then and tossed her head, *you've always dealt with it before, do so again, Arizona!*

She held out her hand. 'A businesslike handshake, Declan? Why not.'

He took her hand but didn't shake it. Instead, he examined it thoughtfully and said finally, 'An elegant hand, Arizona. But I'm glad you don't go in for long, talon-like nails.'

She looked at her short, oval, unvarnished nails and grimaced, taken a bit by surprise. 'They're not exactly practical, long nails, are they?'

'Many women have them, however.'

'I would have thought . . .' She stopped.

'Go on,' he prompted.

'I would have thought you liked your women ultra-sophisticated, Declan,' she said deliberately.

He smiled enigmatically. 'Which just goes to show you shouldn't have too many preconceived ideas about me, Arizona. Mind you, I've seen you looking pretty sophisticated at times.'

She grimaced. 'Sophisticated clothes, perhaps. But since I'm happiest when I'm gardening or making plans for this place or with the kids, I don't think I'm particularly sophisticated at all.' She stopped rather suddenly and looked defiant first then weary.

'What?' he said softly.

'Didn't I give myself away—*making plans for this place*,' she repeated ironically.

'A little,' he said reflectively, 'but I'd always rather you were honest with me, Arizona, so don't worry about it too much.' And so saying, he raised her hand to his lips and kissed it.

Arizona was frozen for a long, strange moment during which she was assaulted by the oddest sensations. She seemed to tingle all the way up her arm. If she'd thought she was conscious of Declan Holmes before, she was doubly so now, and she got the unnerving impression that if he chose to draw her into his arms, she'd be unable to resist.

What did happen was that the door opened and Ben stood there, damp, windblown and breathless, and he took one look at the frozen little scene before his eyes and said in a voice quite unlike his own, 'Let her go, damn you, Declan! I *knew* that's what you were here for, but she was my father's *wife*.'

'Ben!' Arizona protested, as Declan released her hand unhurriedly. 'Ben, what are you doing here anyway? You—'

'You thought I'd be well out of the way, didn't you, Arizona? Well, I couldn't stand those stupid boys so I came back.' And with a furious gesture he turned and flung out of the room, slamming the door.

'Ben!' Arizona whispered and turned to Declan Holmes. 'Now look what you've done!'

'Something that doesn't quite meet the eye?' he suggested with his own eyes narrowed and thoughtful. 'If he's run away from his troop, is there any way you can get in touch with them to let them know he's safe?'

'I . . . yes,' Arizona said agitatedly. 'They have a mobile phone with them that they operate from the battery of their vehicle, only I can't remember where I put the slip of paper . . .' She looked around feverishly then took hold. 'I know where it is—I'll ring them. But what are we going to do with him? He—'

'Leave him to me,' Declan said evenly. He added, 'Don't go to bed until I see you again, Arizona.'

She opened her mouth to say something angry but changed her mind at his look and turned away as he strode out.

It was an hour before he came back to her, during which she'd been able to settle to nothing, and she was sitting disconsolately drinking another cup of coffee.

'How is he? Is he all right? You weren't too hard on him, were you?'

He answered none of her questions as he closed the door and poured himself a cup of coffee.

'Well?' Arizona said impatiently.

'Calm yourself, my dear,' he murmured. 'He's fine—or rather, he will be fine soon. I made a suggestion to him that will, I think, solve a lot of his problems.'

'What?'

'Boarding school.'

'No! Don't you think he's feeling lonely enough as it is without being sent away from us? And then there's Daintry—'

'He can take Daintry. The school I have in mind, as well as being a particularly good school, has a riding school attached.'

'But—'

'Just listen to me, Arizona,' Declan Holmes commanded and waited pointedly.

'Go on,' she said with a shrug after their gazes locked and she detected a will in this matter stronger than her own.

'Thank you,' he said with irony. 'He can come home for the weekend once a month and we can visit him one Sunday a month.'

'It sounds as if we're putting him in jail,' she commented curtly.

'What we'll be doing, in fact, is putting him in the company of other boys his age, providing him with a first-class education, plenty of sport and little time to—mope.'

Arizona stood up. 'I still don't like the thought of it one little bit.'

'Then let me tell you what else we'll be doing for him,' he said dryly. 'I hadn't wanted to go into this and I promised him I wouldn't so *you'll* have to act as if you don't know, but we'll be removing him from the sheer torment of your presence.'

Arizona turned and stared incredulously at Declan Holmes. 'What do you mean?' she whispered.

'I mean that Ben is wildly, miserably and hopelessly in love with you, my dear Arizona, or thinks he is.'

She gasped and paled. 'I . . . he *told* you this?'

'Yes, but only because I suspected it and—' he gestured '—brought the subject up.'

Arizona sat down abruptly. 'But he's only a boy!'

'He's fifteen, Arizona, and I can assure you it's neither impossible nor anything particularly unusual.'

She blinked rapidly. 'But—I feel terrible!'

Declan Holmes smiled slightly. 'It's not your fault. But do you see now why he'll be much better off at boarding school?'

'I suppose so,' she said miserably then looked at Declan suddenly. 'What does *he* think, though?'

He shrugged. 'He's not exactly jumping for joy at the moment, but I think it's helped to have a man-to-man chat, and I promise you, he'll be fine.'

'A man-to-man chat,' she echoed.

'Yes.' He grimaced. 'I told him I was in a similar position.'

She stared at him and felt herself colour. 'Not wildly, miserably, hopelessly in love with me, surely!' she said to cover it.

He returned her look with a little glint in his eyes of wicked amusement. 'I told him I was greatly attracted and planned to marry you—after the first shock of it and after relieving himself of some bitter sentiments on the subject, we discussed it more rationally. I don't suppose he'll get over you immediately, Arizona, but he's at least admitted to himself now that it's out of the question.'

'And he doesn't—hate you?'

'No—would you like him to?'

'Of course not! I just...' She looked confused and exasperated.

'Don't understand men?' he said with a genuine grin. 'He is only fifteen, not too young to think he's in love but young enough for someone like me to be firm but understanding with him. I'm quite sure that before long a girl of his own age will come along and...'

'Oh, I do hope so,' Arizona said fervently. 'Poor Ben.'

Declan Holmes raised a wry eyebrow at her. 'No spare sympathy for me? Considering that we were more or less in the same boat.'

She tightened her lips and started to say something scathing but stopped as she was attacked by another thought. 'So he knows—that means they'll all know by tomorrow!'

He regarded her narrowly. 'Yes. But they had to know sooner or later. Why does it suddenly upset you, Arizona?'

'Because I feel more trapped than ever.' The words were out before she could stop them, and she saw his eyes change and harden. 'I mean—' But she couldn't go on, and she was suddenly claimed by exhausted frustration so that the only thing to do was turn and walk out. He didn't attempt to detain her.

CHAPTER THREE

THEY had a custom, she and Cloris, that on Saturday mornings, Cloris brought her tea and toast in bed, and on Sunday mornings she did the same for Cloris. Not that Arizona took the opportunity to rise late often on Saturdays, but Cloris very much enjoyed being cosseted on a Sunday morning and having the opportunity to read the Sunday papers that were delivered early in peace.

But on this Saturday when Cloris came with her tea, Arizona woke from a deep sleep after spending most of the night tossing and turning, felt dreadful and unwisely mentioned this to Cloris while she was still half asleep then said that she wouldn't be down early if Cloris could hold the fort.

The result of this was that ten minutes later there was a knock on her door. She called out wearily to come in, expecting one of the children, but it was Declan Holmes who did.

She was lying back against the pillows with her knees drawn up and her cup of tea in her hands resting on them, and for a moment she stared at him, stunned. He wore jeans, a khaki shirt with patch pockets and short brown riding boots, he was shaved, his thick dark hair was still damp from the shower and he looked alert but inscrutable.

'What are you doing here?' she got out at last as their gazes clashed.

'Morning, Arizona,' he replied, his blue gaze drifting from her unbrushed hair looped behind her ears to her pink cotton nightshirt with a teddy bear's picnic on the front, then moving briefly around the lovely room. 'What's wrong with you?' he added.

Her lips parted and she frowned. 'Nothing's wrong with me and I don't know why you feel you have the right to—'

'Then why is Cloris convinced you're sickening for something?' he broke in.

Arizona closed her eyes. 'I didn't tell her I was feeling *sick*!'

'She said you said you were feeling dreadful and that it was quite unlike you to want to stay in bed and she's wondering whether she should ring the doctor.'

Arizona muttered something inaudible then took a deep breath and gazed bitterly at Declan Holmes. 'I don't know how I put up with her sometimes.'

His lips twisted in a faint smile. 'She has your best interests at heart.'

'I *know* that. I...' She tailed off frustratedly.

'So you didn't tell her you were feeling dreadful and wanted to stay in bed?'

'Yes...no...I mean, yes, I did, but not because— look, I'm fine,' she said coldly, 'and I don't appreciate your being here like this, so—'

'Then if it's not your health—' he overrode her coolly '—you've been working yourself into a state about this self-imposed trap you're walking into. Is that it, Arizona?' he drawled, his eyes curiously mocking. 'May I give you some advice?'

She opened her mouth, closed it then said wearily, 'I don't suppose I can stop you. Just don't expect me to act on it, Declan.'

He paused, glanced out of the window and said as if changing topics, 'It's a beautiful morning, Arizona. The rain has gone, the ground is steaming gently in clear bright sunshine and smelling delicious. Two horses are saddled, moreover, as eager to have a good gallop before breakfast as I am, and you would be, too—if you weren't lying in bed feeling sorry for yourself and building *traps*,' he said softly and significantly.

Arizona put her cup down, tossed aside the bed-clothes and sprang up. 'Go away!' she commanded. 'I will not be treated like this.'

He looked her up and down, and his gaze lingered on the long expanse of slim legs her nightshirt exposed. 'Like a child?' he suggested gently, his eyes coming back to hers. 'Then why don't you stop behaving like one? Do you always wear teddy bears to bed?' he added quizzically and went on thoughtfully. 'I would have imagined you in something sexier, to go with your lovely bedroom.'

'I've told you once, go away,' Arizona said through her teeth.

He shrugged and looked amused. 'Only if you'll come riding with me.'

'Now it wasn't such a bad idea after all.'

They had dismounted at the cliff top above the beach, and their horses were cropping the grass. It had been a good gallop, and he'd been right about the sheer magic of the morning.

Arizona was sitting on the turf, staring out to sea, a glittering, dancing sea. 'No,' she said briefly.

'Not still sulking?' he murmured and sat down beside her.

She shrugged and thought a little dismally that she probably was but then again, didn't she have cause? She decided to opt for honesty. 'Most victims of blackmail probably don't like it.'

'Even when the results are this pleasant?' He raised a wry eyebrow at her.

'That sounds as if you're a great believer in the end justifying the means,' she countered.

He grinned. 'In this case, yes.'

'Is that how you've got where you are?'

'Are you asking me whether I'm unscrupulous and immoral, Arizona?' he queried gravely.

'Yes,' she said baldly.

'No, I'm not.'

She glanced at him through her lashes, but that was a mistake, she discovered, as she encountered a grave blue gaze that didn't for one moment hide from her the fact that he was laughing at her inwardly.

She looked away. 'That's easy enough to say.'

'True,' he agreed blandly.

'And not so easy to believe, particularly in light of your dealings with me,' she murmured.

'On the contrary, I feel I'm being highly honourable in my dealings with you. And before you say that I'm forcing you to marry me, Arizona—'

'You are.'

'With your connivance, my dear,' he drawled. 'Also your hidden interest, to yourself, that is. Do you know what Cloris said to me when she heard the news?'

Arizona turned to him quite openly this time but once again looked stunned. 'She knows!'

'She knows,' he agreed.

'How? Has Ben—but he wasn't up! None of the kids were.'

'I told her. And what she said was this—that she'd thought it might be on the cards, that she was very happy for us both, that she thought I was the ideal person for you and she had the feeling you thought so too but you were a very stubborn person so not to feel too downhearted if you proved a little difficult.'

'Of all the . . . I don't believe it!'

'Her exact words,' Declan assured her. 'Well, interspersed with typical Cloris kind of stops and starts. She must have sensed,' he added, 'your interest.'

'I don't at all see how she could have,' Arizona said moodily. 'It was all I could do not to let on how much I disliked you.'

'Maybe it was just that, an irrational sort of dislike that made no sense. Perhaps that's what alerted her.'

Arizona lay back on the thick turf disgustedly. 'The whole business annoys me intensely,' she said tautly.

He smiled unexpectedly. 'That's what I like about you, Arizona. One of the things.'

'What?' she asked irritably as he said no more. 'That I get annoyed? I wouldn't have thought it was an asset in a wife at all.'

'Oh, it has its moments. You're not dull to be with .'

'I—' But she stopped abruptly as he propped himself on his elbow beside her and stared into her eyes.

'You?' he murmured with a wryly raised eyebrow.

'Nothing,' she said shortly and would have moved away if a curious sense of, as it turned out, misplaced bravado hadn't claimed her.

'May I make another suggestion?' he said after a minute or two.

'Seeing as you're so full of them this morning, why not?'

'Here goes then,' he said with a humorous quirk to his lips. 'Now we've had a little spat, well, two, and it is only eight o'clock in the morning, now you've done that and done yourself proud, so to speak, don't you think it would be all right to let yourself relax a little and—go with the flow? For a while at least?'

'That's the most illogical thing I've heard! It's worse, it's insulting!'

'Depends how you take it.'

'No! I mean there is no other way to take it. You're saying in effect that . . .' Words failed her.

'All I'm saying is, until you relax and try it, you really don't know what you're fighting about.'

'Try being kissed by you?' she suggested ominously.

'Uh-huh.'

'You never let up, do you?'

'I thought we'd established that.'

'All right,' she said abruptly, 'then let's establish something else—go ahead.' She closed her eyes and lay still.

'I hesitate to disturb you, Arizona,' he said quite gently after a pause, 'but you look a bit ridiculous.'

Her lashes flew up and her grey eyes flashed. 'How dare you? You—'

'You keeping saying that to me,' he murmured.

She sat up, her cheeks flooded with colour but her eyes just as angry, then she sprang up and caught her poor horse, taking it quite unawares, and swung herself into the saddle. She also yelled something pithy and highly uncomplimentary to Declan Holmes as she galloped off, and heard him laughing at her clearly.

*   *   *

Breakfast was awaiting her in the kitchen. The children had theirs, Cloris informed her, and Ben had got away safely.

'Got away? Where?' Arizona said bewilderedly.

'Didn't Mr. Holmes tell you?'

'No, Cloris, he did not!'

Cloris shrugged. 'He arranged for him to spend the weekend in Sydney with some friends of his. They have a yacht and a boy Ben's age—he knows him, so that's what they'll be doing this weekend, sailing. I do think it was a lovely thing to do for Ben, don't you, Arizona? He does need something to take him out of himself at the moment.'

'But how did he get—'

'I arranged for a car to come down and pick him up,' Declan Holmes said smoothly, coming in through the back door.

'You might have told me,' Arizona protested, still feeling enraged and embarrassed.

'Slipped my mind.' He sat down at the kitchen table. 'I'm starving.'

Cloris glowed. 'Well, I've got a lovely breakfast for you, Mr. Holmes. Do sit down, Arizona, it's your favourite, too. You're looking much better!'

Arizona took a deep breath—and sat down. Cloris bustled about for a few minutes then produced perfectly cooked bacon and eggs with fried tomatoes and banana. It was as she poured their coffee that she produced her second bombshell. 'Goodness me!' she exclaimed. 'I don't know where my wits are this morning. Rosemary Hickson called, Arizona, to remind you of her dinner party tonight. I told her it was just as well she had called because I'd forgotten and I thought you might have, too. But I explained why,' she added anxiously.

Arizona took another deep breath. 'Why?'

'Why what?' Cloris looked at her, perplexed, and Declan ate the last of his breakfast serenely.

'Why would we have forgotten, Cloris?' Arizona said deliberately.

'Oh, hadn't you, Arizona? I thought you must have because you were talking about a bonfire tonight—'

'Cloris, I *had* forgotten,' Arizona said, goaded, 'as you very well know, but the why is what I'm trying to establish!'

'Oh, that!' Cloris brightened. 'Because of Mr. Holmes coming to stay unexpectedly, of course—not to mention, well, other things, but,' she said hastily, 'when I told Mrs. Hickson, she said it wasn't a problem. In fact she said she'd be thrilled to have you to dinner tonight, Mr. Holmes. She said it would even up her table delightfully.' Cloris paused, eyed Arizona nervously then suddenly came round the table and put her arms around her. 'I'm so happy for you, pet, I know I sometimes can be trying and—well, all the same, I often think of you as a daughter, you've been so very, very good to the children and I hope you'll be very, very happy.' She withdrew her arms and wiped a tear from her cheek.

Arizona stared at her, thought, *Oh, hell, I feel like a real heel!* And put her arms around Cloris, saying huskily, 'Thank you, I love you, too, you know, and I'm sure that of the two of us, I'm the trying one.'

'Your Saturdays are pretty busy,' Declan Holmes said as he steered the Saab towards the Hickson property, which adjoined Scawfell.

Arizona shrugged.

'What with pony club, Brownies et al., I'm surprised you're not exhausted,' he added and glanced sideways at her.

Arizona smoothed the short skirt of her yellow silk cocktail dress. The Hicksons always dressed formally for their dinner parties, and she'd put up her hair. She wore sheer pale nylons and grey kid high-heeled shoes. She also said witheringly, 'Well, I'm not. Physically, that is.'

'But you're all tense and wrought up mentally,' he commented dryly. 'It shows.'

Arizona laid her head back with a sudden little sigh. 'Yes. Mightn't you be if you were in my shoes?'

'If I knew a bit more about you and why you're so determined to hate me but still marry me, perhaps I could answer that.'

Arizona closed her eyes briefly. 'Never mind, just take it as read,' she said wearily. 'Are you going to break the news to the Hicksons, as well?'

'Would you like me to?'

'No.'

'Then I won't,' he said mildly. 'We're nearly there. From what I remember, Rosemary Hickson is an overwhelming, high-powered blonde.'

'You're not wrong—but she's been a good friend,' Arizona added thoughtfully. Then she said on a downbeat, 'We are here.'

He stopped the car, but before he switched the engine off, he put a hand over hers and said surprisingly, 'Look at it this way for a change, Arizona. You're quite stunning, you have an unusual and beautiful name, you're young, spirited and intelligent, you smell delicious—why not drop the weight of the world off your shoulders for an evening?'

Her eyes flew to his full of puzzled surprise. 'I—'

'Just give it a try.' And he turned the key off, got out and came round to open the door for her. Arizona hesitated then swung her legs out, saw the way his blue gaze lingered on them then met her eyes expressionlessly—and she found herself looking away with a curious tingling of her nerves.

'Darling, so lovely to see you!' Rosemary Hickson gushed, as usual sporting her impressive bust in a very low-cut black dress. 'And how are you, Declan—we have met before, so delightful to have you both, especially—' she lowered her voice fractionally '—in view of the good tidings Cloris passed on this morning, although she did make me promise not to mention it—she wasn't sure she should have said anything, you see, so I haven't said a word to anyone else!'

Grey eyes met blue ones, and for a second outrage glinted in Arizona's gaze but then—perhaps it all just become too much? she wondered—she found herself laughing just a touch hysterically. And felt Declan's hand enclose her own as he said gravely, 'How are you, Rosemary? Thank you for inviting me, and if you wouldn't mind, we'd like to keep our engagement a secret for a bit longer.'

'Of course! Of course! But I'm thrilled to be one of the first in the know. Now come and meet everyone—we're twelve tonight so we should have great fun.'

But as she turned to lead the way, Declan held Arizona back for a moment and said very quietly, 'All right?'

'I...I'm working on it. Perhaps I will do as you suggested in the car.'

'Good girl.'

'Not so bad, was it?'

Arizona laid her head back against the leather car seat. 'That's the second time you've said that to me today.'

'Was it?'

'No.' She closed her eyes and thought over the evening. Peter had designed the Hicksons' home, so it was elegant and beautifully appointed. The food had been superb, the company entertaining and by some mysterious means, she'd transformed herself into the person Declan had advised her to be—untouched by the weight of the world, good company although with just a hint of reserve at times when she became conscious of the admiration she saw in the men's eyes and the speculation she saw amongst the women of the party concerning her relationship with Declan. But for the most part it had been a relaxed evening for her, and she might have been not a widow with four stepchildren but the youngest member of the company who had charmed and held her own. 'I feel like Cinderella now, however,' she murmured involuntarily.

'Thanks,' he said dryly.

She glanced at him briefly. 'Sorry, I should be thanking you for—well, I don't quite know what, but I guess for bringing out the best in me for a while.'

'Do you really mean that, Arizona?'

'Yes, surprisingly I do,' she murmured. 'It's a pity it can't last.'

He pulled the car up in front of the house and turned to her. 'It could, you know,' he said quietly. 'Take your shoes off and come for a walk with me. Just down the lawn to the cliff. If nothing else it will help dispose of a very rich meal.'

'To around about the same spot where I made myself ridiculous this morning?' she queried wearily.

'Perhaps the moonlight on the sea and a clear, scented, beautiful night will help you to be less so.'

'I wonder,' she said barely audibly, dropped her face into her hands for a second then kicked off her shoes. 'Okay, you're on,' she added with something more like defiance, and she got out of the car and started to stride across the lawn in her stockinged feet.

He caught up with her halfway to the cliff top and took her hand, resisting her attempt to pull away saying abruptly, 'Stop it, Arizona.'

So she slowed with a show of obedience that was a mockery but said nothing. And he was right, when they got there, the moon was shining on a pewter sea and picking the crescent of beach up below, turning it to a dazzling white. There were night scents on the air, honeysuckle and jasmine mingled with the sea air, dew-damp grass.

'It is . . . it is lovely,' she said shakenly after they'd said nothing for long minutes, just drunk it all in. 'Now do you understand why I'm marrying you, Declan?'

He hadn't let go of her hand and his grasp tightened fractionally. 'Is that why you married Pete? For Scawfell?'

'Of course, I thought you knew. And his money.' Her voice still shook slightly. 'Although I may have miscalculated there.'

'What about this?' He released her but put his hands on her shoulders and stared at her narrowly. 'This,' he repeated very quietly and steadily. 'Having a man run his hands over your skin.' He did so, down her arms and back again, then slid his long fingers beneath the straps of her dress. 'Being held and having your breasts touched, your nipples stroked, your beautiful mouth claimed.' And he did just that, drew his hands down the front of her dress to cup her breasts and run his thumbs over her nipples beneath the yellow silk and the lace of her bra—and as they hardened and she breathed erratically, he tantalisingly slid his hands away, around her waist, and pulled her closer so he could kiss her lips.

She kept them stubbornly closed then parted them involuntarily as his hands moved again, to her hips, to trace the outline of her bikini briefs beneath the thin silk, exploring, stroking, moulding her to him at the same time. He bent his head then and started to kiss her deeply.

It was, as she'd always feared and suspected it would be, impossible to remain unaffected. There was between them a surge of sheer magnetism, a physical match between the tall hard planes of his body and the soft curves of her own despite or perhaps even heightened by their mutual animosity. And it had been there ever since the first time she'd found him watching her out of those clever, sometimes so cynical blue eyes.

How can I handle this, she found herself thinking chaotically, *when I don't even know what it is, love or hate, a new war or—but I must.* And she managed at last to draw away, although not completely. He allowed her to rest against the circle of his arms and take several unsteady breaths before she murmured ingenuously, 'Oh, yes, but I must say I hadn't expected you to be so expert, Declan. I'm quite impressed—yes, *quite* impressed.'

Oddly enough, it gave her no satisfaction that he called her a bitch then in cold clinical tones and released her. In fact, instead, she felt something shrivel inside her, although she said, albeit a bit raggedly, 'But you knew that, too, didn't you—do you still want to marry me? I'll understand if you've changed your mind. You know, I've been thinking, if you kept Scawfell for the children, you could always keep me on instead of getting them a new governess. After all, that seems to be the one thing you admire me for—'

She stopped because he'd turned away from her for most of her speech but he turned back and for a moment she was frightened by what she saw in his eyes. But he said almost leisurely, 'Oh, no, Arizona. If you want Scawfell and the children, it has to be on my terms or not at all.'

'But I don't understand.' She stopped again as she heard the note of fear in her voice. 'I mean . . . why?' And heard something else in her voice that made her cringe inwardly, a sort of desperate uncertainty.

He laughed softly. 'For the pleasure of bringing you to your knees, for one thing, Arizona. You see,' he drawled, 'you've resisted all my efforts to make some sense of this, so I'm afraid that now, my dear, you're going to have to put up with the consequences—me and Scawfell. Or nothing.'

And he walked towards the house without a backward glance.

She was awoken the next morning by Sarah and Richard leaping onto her bed. 'What the ... what are you doing?' she said groggily.

'Waking you up, sleepyhead!' Sarah replied obligingly.

Her twin brother added, 'It's six o'clock!'

Arizona groaned as they slipped in on either side of her. 'It's also Sunday! What have I done to deserve this on a Sunday morning?'

They giggled and enveloped her in a bear hug, and Declan walked in on them.

Arizona froze but the twins released her and sat up interestedly. 'Hi, Declan,' they chorused, and Richard said, 'We were wondering, since you're going to marry Arizona, what we should call you. I mean is it okay to go on calling you Declan?'

'Because we don't think we should call you Dad really,' Sarah said.

'Declan will do fine,' he murmured. 'Do you always wake Arizona up at this ungodly hour of the day?'

'Well, you're here, too,' Richard pointed out, and Arizona couldn't help the slightly ironic glint that came to her eye as his gaze caught hers.

'I'm here to tell her that Daisy's crying,' he said to the twins, but returned the irony directly to Arizona.

She sat up. 'What—'

'That's what we came to tell her!' Sarah said triumphantly. 'We think she's sick or something.'

'Well, why didn't you say so!' Arizona scrambled out of bed, once again caught in her teddy bear's picnic nightshirt, and was in no way mollified as

Declan reached for the dressing gown lying across the bottom of the bed and handed it to her gravely.

'Daisy—Daisy, darling, what's wrong?' Arizona knelt beside the bed and smoothed Daisy's forehead. Declan and Richard and Sarah stood behind her.

'You're not going to go away, are you, Arizona?' Daisy wound her arms around Arizona's neck and pressed her hot, wet cheek to Arizona's.

'No, Daisy, I told you—'

'Ben's gone,' Daisy wept.

'Only for the weekend, sweetheart, and not because he was cross with you, I promise you.'

'But you're getting married, you told me so yesterday—I don't know what that means—and I feel horrible.'

'Daisy, Daisy,' Arizona said gently and unwound her arms, 'let me have a look at your chest, honey bunch, because I think I may know why you're feeling horrible.' She opened Daisy's pink pyjama jacket, and the rash on her little chest was quite visible. 'Is your throat sore, pet?'

Daisy nodded, still weeping copiously. 'And my head.'

'Measles?' Declan said quietly, behind her.

'Looks like it. She's very hot. Daisy, guess what, I'm going to call Dr. Lakewood, now you like her, don't you? And she'll help us make you feel better.'

'Am I sick?' Daisy said, suddenly looking more alert. 'Sam Johnson had to go home early from school the other day because he was sick.' She sat up with her blonde hair sticking to her forehead, her cheeks flushed but her eyes brighter. 'Will this make me more important? It did for Sam, Teacher made him lie down next to her on a cushion until his mother came!'

'Oh, tremendously important, darling!' Arizona said with a loving smile, while Sarah and Richard cast their eyes heavenwards but came to perch on the end of their little sister's bed.

'You'll have to stay in bed for days, Daisy. We know because we had it when we were six—' Arizona breathed relievedly when Sarah said this '—but we'll read you stories and play games with you.'

'But you'll look after me, won't you, Arizona?' Daisy said anxiously.

'Of course. Don't I always?' Arizona said lightly as she dropped a kiss on her head and stood up. 'Now I'm just going to ring the doctor, then I'll come straight back and make you more comfortable.' But as she turned around, it was to see a curiously intent look in Declan Holmes's eyes as they rested on her. She thought, as she moved past him, *I don't know why you're looking at me like that, but at least I've got something else to think about!*

It was four o'clock in the afternoon before she stopped and sat down to have a cup of tea on the front veranda, where Cloris had set it out on a white-clothed table. Tea and crumpets. Sarah and Richard had homemade lemonade before racing off, leaving her alone with Declan. It was a hot, bright afternoon.

'Phew!' She sat down and lifted her hair off her neck.

'Hot?' he queried and poured her a cup of tea.

'Hot and bothered, but she's asleep now, and a lot less emotional,' she added wryly.

He said nothing.

'Thanks for taking the twins off my hands,' she said a few minutes later.

'Not a problem,' he murmured and smiled suddenly. 'I've had quite an—instructive day. They're inexhaustible, aren't they?'

Arizona laughed. 'You're not wrong. It's strange—' She stopped.

'What is?'

She looked at her cup and cursed herself inwardly for letting her tongue run away with her unwittingly.

'Arizona?' he prompted quietly.

She looked up at last and shrugged. 'I had no idea how I was going to face you today, that's all.'

'Saved by a case of measles, of all things.'

She searched his expression for mockery or irony, but his eyes were enigmatic. 'I guess so,' she said expressionlessly.

'Were you really worried, Arizona?'

She hesitated. 'I couldn't help wondering where we would go from—there.'

'And I couldn't help wondering how much of what you said last night was...believable.'

'Not at the time, you didn't,' she countered dryly then bit her lip.

'True,' he agreed reflectively. 'But when I saw you with Daisy this morning, it struck me that there are two sides of you, Arizona, that don't match at all.'

'Yes, well, that's me,' she tried to say flippantly and moved restlessly.

'Tell me some more about your mother.' He stretched his long legs out and clasped his hands behind his head.

'No.'

He raised his eyebrows quizzically. 'I can always find out.'

A glint of anger lit her grey eyes. 'How despicable,' she taunted.

'Not if there's some deep dark mystery—'

'There's not. She was simply a...rather foolish woman, and I have no ambition to follow in her footsteps,' Arizona said abruptly.

'Do you mean she threw everything up for love and suffered accordingly?' he hazarded. 'Is that why you thought you'd do things the other way around?'

'Now why would I imagine you'd believe anything else?' she marvelled.

'Well, until you tell me otherwise, what am I supposed to believe?' he drawled.

'All right, yes,' she said moodily.

'So you hate your mother,' he said after a pause.

'No, I don't.'

'Do you keep in touch with her?'

'Yes, I do. But, thank heavens, she's somewhere even you would have difficulty finding—look, how are we going to go on?' she asked curtly.

'I don't have any change of plan in mind. Do you?' he queried politely.

'You seem to forget, I'm the one with little choice, Declan,' she replied with considerable irony.

'So you are, Arizona, so you are.'

'Oh, this is impossible.' She jumped up and was horrified to discover she had tears on her lashes.

He got up smoothly. 'Then let me make another suggestion.' He took her hand and forced her to face him.

'You're hurting me,' she said proudly, despite those suspicious tears.

'Only because you're asking for it,' he countered coolly, 'so just stand still and listen to me for a change.'

'Aye, aye, sir!'

His mouth hardened for a moment then he relaxed and laughed softly. 'Anyone would think I was about to attack you,' he said lazily. 'I can assure you I'm not. I'm equally sure after last night that it will never have to come to that—but it was nothing,' he said as she gasped, 'along those lines at all, Arizona.' His blue eyes mocked her. 'I was merely going to suggest,' he continued smoothly, 'that while you had your hands full with Daisy, I go back to Sydney this afternoon, pick Ben up and spend a few days with him.'

'Ben!' Arizona said huskily and put her free hand to her brow, a bit dazed. 'I haven't even had time to think about him today. But—what would you do with him?'

'Take him to see the school I have in mind and—' he shrugged '—just do a few of the things fifteen-year-old boys might enjoy.'

'Would . . . would you?' she said uncertainly.

'Contrary to your opinion of me, Arizona,' he drawled, 'I'm not a monster.'

'I didn't think you were in that respect,' she said irritably. 'But you are a super, high-powered businessman—or aren't you?'

'I'm on holiday,' he reminded her softly and stared into her eyes deliberately.

'Well—' she had the grace to colour faintly '—I'm sorry...but that would be—I'd be very grateful if you would.'

'Thank you. For the apology,' he murmured.

The colour in her cheeks grew and she tried to turn away but he wouldn't let her. 'There's just one thing I'd like you to do while I'm away, Arizona,' he went on. 'And that's to make up your mind about yourself.'

'What do you mean?' She frowned at him.

'You see,' he explained gravely, 'I'm getting these confused signals. Last night you went out of your way to be a fortune-huntress and a vamp, although for a while you kissed me like a girl who was rather overcome, even a little in love... I find that strange, Arizona, don't you?'

She stared into his eyes and felt like a butterfly pinned to a cloth. She licked her lips and opened her mouth to speak, but he smiled, unamused, and released her hand to put a finger on her lips. 'No. I'd rather you thought about it instead of launching into a tirade of some kind. And of course, for my part, there'll be the sense of anticipation, while we're apart, as to what you'll be when I return. The vamp?' he mused. 'The cold-hearted gold-digger? Or simply an angry and confused young woman but at least an honest one?'

CHAPTER FOUR

HE WAS away for four days.

Days of inner turmoil for Arizona, which she would have loved to try to combat by being furiously busy but spent mostly with Daisy. The result was that at night, with Daisy tucked up and sleeping peacefully, she wasn't physically tired herself and had plenty of time to ponder on the nature of her dilemma, and Declan Holmes's acuteness... *Not that I'm in love with him,* she told herself repeatedly, *but there's no doubt I was a bit overcome.* She shivered in sudden remembrance. *There's no doubt he intrigues me as no man ever has, but at the same time he engenders this raging hostility in me! The thing is—who's to blame for that? I haven't been honest with him for a very good reason, but why should I? He certainly started out believing the worst of me. Why does he really want to marry me, then? It has to be revenge because I wouldn't look at him when Pete was alive or—afterwards, he as good as said so that awful night. But what does that make him?*

'I don't know,' she said aloud to herself in the dark, in bed one night. 'That's the thing, I don't know. What kind of a man goes to these lengths over a wife of a friend, a wife who did the right thing? Is it because *afterwards*, I was still determined to have nothing to do with him? How could he know that in spite of the way I was, it was there, this... curiosity, this... Will it never leave me?' she wondered still aloud and desolately, and turned to hide her suddenly hot face in the pillow. *But then he can be nice,* she thought, some minutes later, *and good with the kids but all the same he's using them . . .*

How can I leave them? she asked herself another night. *Especially Daisy. I'd never forgive myself, I've promised . . . so I've got to work something out but it's unbelievable all the same. Or is it, Arizona,* she asked herself bleakly, and lay quite still thinking of how he'd kissed her, how it had overcome her, and wondering what it would be like to be married to a man you didn't understand, a man who you knew wanted you but had no idea how he would use you . . .

They came back on a Thursday afternoon, catching Arizona unawares. Daisy was up and having some fresh air, wearing a pair of sunglasses and looking much better. They were on the veranda doing a jigsaw puzzle. As soon as she saw the car and then Ben getting out, Daisy jumped up ecstatically, knocking the puzzle off the table, and dashed down the steps, calling his name.

'Ben, Ben, I've been sick and very important but I'm better now. Oh, Ben, you did come back—Arizona told me not to lecture you any more so I won't!'

Ben grinned and picked her up. 'Believe it or not, I missed you, Bubbles,' he said affectionately, using his pet name for her, and Arizona relaxed a bit because this was more like the old Ben. But she thought she detected a slight constraint as he came up the steps with his eyes not quite meeting hers as he still carried Daisy, and she breathed deeply.

'Ben,' she said with a grin of her own, 'I hope
you've had measles in case it's still lingering. Did you
have a good time? We missed you, too.'

And she thought she must have pulled it off, that
it must have come out easily and naturally because
she saw Ben visibly relax, and he said enthusiastically,
'I had a ball!'

Then the twins streaked round the corner of the
house and they flowed inside together in one noisy,
happy group. Arizona bent to gather up the puzzle.

'Here, let me give you a hand.'

'Thanks,' she said to Declan as he knelt beside her,
and that was all they said until every last piece of
puzzle had been retrieved.

'How are you?' he queried when they stood up at
last.

'Fine, thanks,' she answered but didn't know if it
was true because she was still curiously affected by
the accidental touching of his hand on hers as they'd
sought for the same piece.

'You don't altogether look it,' he murmured, his
brows drawn together in a faint frown.

'Well, I am, really,' she tried to say lightly. And
because she felt she needed to emphasize that it was
nothing to do with him, she added, 'Just a bit housebound at present, that's all.'

'Would you let me take you out to dinner tonight
then?'

'Oh, no.' She smiled perfunctorily. 'Daisy's much
better, I'll be able to get out and about soon, and Ben
looks so much better, too, thank you for that!' She
was aware as soon as she stopped speaking, that she'd
sounded stilted and harassed, and bit her lip.

'Would dinner out alone with me be so much worse than dinner here with me?'

'I didn't mean that—'

'Yes, you did, Arizona,' he contradicted coolly.

Her shoulders slumped suddenly. 'All right, so what if I did,' she murmured, barely audibly. 'Anyway, Daisy is still—'

'Daisy's much better, you said so yourself, she's got Ben, the twins and Cloris. And much as I appreciate your concern for her, we shouldn't allow this fear she has of being deserted to get out of hand.'

Of course he's right about that, she thought dismally, *and anyway I did decide to level with him, didn't I? Is there any point in trying to put it off?*

'You've won,' she said with an odd little sigh. 'What time shall we go?'

'About seven,' he said slowly, his eyes narrowed. 'I thought we might try Zena's in the village.' The village was the nearest town in the area, about ten miles away. 'Rosemary gave it quite a wrap the other night, if you recall.'

'Rosemary should know!'

'I thought you liked Rosemary,' he murmured.

'I do.' Arizona grimaced wryly. 'That doesn't blind me to the fact that Rosemary has an uncanny knack of always finding the most exclusive and *expensive* places around.'

His lips twisted. 'Exclusive?'

She shrugged. 'The kind of places you're liable to meet all the best people, of the same social calibre, same old schools, similar financial standing—that kind of thing. Although not necessarily the best food.'

He looked amused. 'Are you really objecting to that, or is it the thought of being seen with me by people who may recognize us?'

'Not at all.' She stared at him scornfully.

'That's more my Arizona,' he reflected. 'Do you have a better suggestion, then?'

She tried to contain her irritation but knew she was on her mettle as she said carefully, 'There's an old pub on the edge of town with a garden that overlooks the sea. A lot of the local fishermen patronize it because they serve the best and freshest lobster, oysters and prawns around, and you can eat outside, but it has absolutely no social pretensions whatever—a lot of its patrons barely made high school.'

'Well, you win this time, my dear,' he drawled, but as she stiffened he added, 'as a matter of fact it sounds much better.'

'You won't find any fancy French wines there,' she warned. 'More like cheap plonk.'

'Who cares?' he replied. 'It's the food that counts.'

She was astounded by the difference in her when they left, and more so when they entered the pub. She hadn't dressed up, although she did wear beautifully tailored jeans, flat navy suede shoes and a white top with padded shoulders made from a bubble-knit material that was at the same time simple, stylish and warm. She had also washed her hair and tied it back, dark, gold-streaked and shining, at her nape, with a navy blue scarf, and touched mascara to her lashes and a deep bronze colour to her lips.

Her sense of well-being had started as they left, when Declan had firmly but kindly told all and sundry he was taking her out to dinner but they'd be back in a couple of hours. Daisy had not so much as blinked an eyelid, and Ben had looked quite unaffected. Arizona had had to admit that this *had* caused her a mental raising of her eyebrows along the lines of how some men simply had this habit of command and how annoyingly effective it was, but she couldn't hold the cynicism of the thought for long. Not as they left the house behind, drove beyond Scawfell's fences and on to the moonlight-washed road. *Perhaps I do need a break,* she thought ruefully.

Then, as she walked through the pub and a sudden, stunned silence fell as all in the place took in her shining hair, her clear pale skin, her figure, she suddenly felt tall, lithe, elegant—and confident.

'Well,' Declan Holmes said with a curious little smile playing on his lips as he found them a table in the garden and drew out a chair for her, 'you certainly cut a swathe through that lot.'

'Didn't mean to,' she said wryly.

'But you enjoyed it?' he suggested, sitting down himself.

'I cannot tell a lie.' She smiled faintly. 'It worked wonders for my ego.' She sobered and started to look for hidden meanings in his words. 'If that makes me a vamp or—'

'Not at all—just refreshingly human and honestly female.'

'Do you mean that?' she asked abruptly.

'Yes,' he said simply.

Arizona sat back a bit stumped.

'What I'd like to know now,' he said after a pause, and she tensed slightly, which he saw and acknowledged with a twist of his lips, 'is whether someone will come to serve us or whether I have to go inside

to order our meal, leaving you out here alone, which
is something I'm not altogether keen to do—I'm sure
there are at least fifty men around who would be only
too happy to take my place.'

She relaxed and grinned. 'Someone will come for
our order, I'm only too happy to tell you.'

'At least—' he paused '—you feel safe with me,
Arizona. That has to mean something—no, don't
tense up, let's enjoy this meal in some sort of
friendship.'

So they ate delicous, plump little oysters *naturel*,
and mouth-watering lobster grilled with butter on a
bed of rice and accompanied by a crisp side salad.
Declan ordered a carafe of house wine, probably out
of a cask, she warned, but it turned out to be quite
a pleasant moselle. And once again they were assailed
by a variety of perfumes from the garden around them
and the sound of waves on the shore not far away.

'Thanks,' she said pushing her lobster plate away
at last and touching a paper napkin to her lips,
whereas Zena's would have had fine linen, 'that was
not only delicious, but I really think I did need to get
away for a while.'

'It was your expertise that brought us here.'

'I was your—something that persuaded me to
come.'

'Does that make us quits?' he speculated idly.

She didn't answer immediately. Then she said,
gathering her resources, 'You told me to do something while you were away. I think I've done it.'

'What?' he asked quietly.

'Decided to tell you some things. I'm not a vamp,
and I'm not really a fortune-huntress. I married Peter
because I trusted him, and I don't usually trust men.
I—married him because it was what he wanted rather

desperately, but I would have been quite happy to stay on as the governess—only once he fell in love with me, I couldn't have. But I was always honest with him, I told him from the beginning that I didn't, couldn't love him the same way, that it didn't seem possible for me to fall in love like that . . . and I hoped it never would.'

'Did you tell him why?' Declan asked after a long pause.

'Yes. Well, he'd begun to guess anyway because of—as he put it—the way I so determinedly froze men off.'

'Are you going to tell me, Arizona?'

'I would rather not,' she said straightly. 'It can't change anything. Could we just leave it at that?'

'I don't think so,' he murmured. 'That's asking a bit much of me, don't you think?'

'All right,' she said abruptly. 'My mother had a few men in her life. Every last one of them deserted her, including my father, throwing her into the depths of despair. I think I was about sixteen when I made a vow no man would do that to me. And I'm sorry to say but there's nothing about you, Declan, that has made me change my mind.'

He smiled slightly. 'Point taken, but let's not jump the gun. Did it never occur to you that your mother may have been at fault at all?'

'Of course it did,' Arizona said briefly then added, 'I'm very much like my mother, to look at, that is.'

'Ah, so it's yourself you don't trust, Arizona?'

'No. But there was something in her that seemed to bring out a fatal urge in men to dominate and discard her, not to mention milk her dry. I . . .' She hesitated. 'I would be foolish to allow that to happen to me, don't you agree?'

'And that's why you opted for a loveless marriage?'

'It wasn't loveless,' she said very quietly. 'I was happy and comfortable with Peter, and because I like to pay my debts, I went out of my way to make him happy,' she added proudly.

'In bed as well as out of it?'

'Yes,' she said after a long pause, during which she studied her hands.

'It was pretty obvious that you fulfilled him—did he do the same for you, Arizona?'

There was a long silence, then she raised her eyes to him at last, and they were expressionless. 'Yes.'

They stared at each other. 'And will you go out of your way to make me happy in that particular way, Arizona?' he said softly but with a wealth of meaning in his tone and the way his eyes roamed over her then.

She shivered and couldn't quite hide it. But she said evenly enough, 'That's the other thing we should discuss. I don't owe you anything, Declan—'

'I agree.'

'So—' She stopped and stared at him. 'What did you say?'

'I agree.'

'Then?' Her eyes were wide and stunned. 'I don't understand what you...why we're...' She couldn't go on.

He sat up and moved his glass on the table. 'I thought we might approach this a bit differently now. On the premise that you *don't* owe me anything, Arizona, but we are caught up in a difficult situation to which the most logical solution is to get married.'

She gazed at him, her lips parted, her eyes bewildered.

'Well, it is, isn't it?' he murmured wryly.

'I don't—'

'You don't see why? Let me tell you,' he drawled. 'You find you can't leave the kids or bear the thought of them being deprived of Scawfell.' He narrowed his eyes then shrugged. 'I've had the evidence of my own eyes,' he said in a different voice, 'as to how genuine you are in these matters, not to mention what a wrench it would be for them. Whereas I—' he paused and grimaced '—find myself in the position, ironically similar to Pete's, as it happens, of not being able to just hand you the place and the kids. That's why there really is only one solution for us,' he said simply.

'I . . .' Once again she got stuck.

'You?'

'Don't know what to say . . .'

'Well, look at it this way.' He sat back and clasped his hands behind his head, 'It would be another marriage of convenience for you. It would have most of the ingredients that made you happy and comfortable before. And has it never occurred to you, Arizona, that you have me as much of a hostage as I may have you?'

'No,' she said dryly.

'Then think about it now,' he suggested. 'Unless you seriously believe I don't have their interests at heart?'

'But—' she licked her lips '—would you be happy with a . . . total marriage of convenience?'

Their gazes caught and held, and she saw a little glint of amusement in his as he said softly, 'Oh, no, but it would lack all the elements of me wanting to dominate and discard you, because of the nature of our—obligations.'

'So—what would it be like?'

'You here, pursuing what you've told me means most to you, me being here when I can, us sleeping together on those occasions and, I hope, fulfilling each other as little or as much as it's in us to do so. You know—' he lowered his arms and grimaced again '—for a girl like you, determined not to fall in love, I would have thought it would have been fairly ideal. You would also have the protection of my name against all the men you have to freeze off so determinedly,' he said gently.

Arizona shivered again but couldn't quite understand why and moved her shoulders restlessly.

'The other thing,' he said evenly, 'is the fact that I do arouse you, my dear. Despite being a despised member of the sex you so mistrust. Are you afraid it will—get out of hand for you?'

Yes, something in her cried, but she could only stare at him bitterly, with images of her mother and other, worse images passing through her mind.

'Then again—' he smiled unexpectedly '—I wouldn't expect our life to be all passing sex and nothing else. I'd like to think once you relaxed a bit about it all there could be some fun and laughter, some happy, good times, too.'

And she was shaken to find no evidence of irony or mockery in his eyes or voice at all.

'What happens—' she cleared her throat '—what happens when they've all grown up and left?'

He stared beyond her for a moment. 'Who knows?'

It was like a blow, she discovered, and might even have flinched unknowingly because he added, 'We might even find we've become a habit with each other.'

Arizona blinked several times, which he watched narrowly. Then he said quietly, 'So, what's it to be, my dear?'

She didn't realize that her shoulders slumped fractionally as she looked away and said, barely audibly, 'Yes...'

He said nothing for so long, she was forced to look at him again, and then all he said was, 'Let's go—I've something to show you.'

He drove them to a spot where the road rounded a headland and there was a viewing verge where he pulled the car up.

'I've seen this view quite often,' Arizona murmured, more for something to say as she stared out over a wrinkled, silver-foil sea beneath a bright moon.

'But you haven't seen this.' He switched on the overhead light and pulled something out of his jacket pocket. A little, midnight-blue velvet box.

Arizona stared at it, knowing immediately what was to come, then switched her gaze to the plain gold wedding ring on her left hand. 'I—'

'Now is the time to take it off, Arizona. Now is the time to lay Pete to rest, finally. After all, if nothing else, we're two people who loved and admired him, two people who have the welfare of his children at heart.'

'I suppose so, when you put it like that...' But a teardrop fell on her hand as she hesitated then slipped the gold band off.

And Declan Holmes flicked the blue velvet box open, drew a sunburst of diamonds out of it, and taking her nerveless left hand, slid the ring onto her finger.

'Thanks,' she said foolishly, examining it with one half of her mind, seeing that it was delicate and exquisite and unusual, three diamonds along the band with two sets of two smaller ones separating them, noting that it was probably priceless and fitted perfectly—and with the other half of her mind curiously numb. 'I'll...look after it.'

'Is that all?' he said wryly.

'Well, what do you want me to say?' Her voice was husky and uncertain.

'I thought there was something we might do.'

She looked across at him swiftly. 'Another moonlight kiss?' she hazarded but without the derision the words were meant to imply. And she closed her eyes, frustrated.

'Why not?' he mocked. 'You didn't mind the last one, once we got going. But let's step outside for a minute or two.'

She got out after him because she couldn't think of what else to do, and they stood side by side against the bonnet of the car and watched as a huge container ship out to sea slid its dark bulk through the water like a wraith but for its lights. 'Red to port, green to starboard,' she murmured.

'You know something about shipping?'

'Not a lot,' she answered. 'It was just something to say. Do you?'

'Yes. I was in the Navy once.'

Surprise caused Arizona to look at him. 'Why?'

'Why?' He grimaced. 'Why not?'

She thought for a moment. 'I don't know. But one sort of thinks of people in the Navy as being dedicated to the sea.'

'I didn't sail ships, I flew helicopters for them. My father thought it would be a good way to combine a love of flying, a bit of fascination for the sea—with some character building. He was probably right.'

'I can't imagine...' Arizona said slowly and stopped. 'I mean—' she tried again '—it's difficult to think of you being dictated to by anyone, even a father—you said that,' she added by way of explanation, 'as if you didn't really agree with him.'

'You're right,' he murmured amusedly, 'there wasn't a lot I agreed with him about—the way he treated my mother and the way he ran the business being the principal disagreements we had. So any of his suggestions were generally anathema to me, but in hindsight,' he mused, 'he was right about the Navy. In so far as it gave me the toughness and maturity to take control eventually and... avert bankruptcy.'

'What did he do?'

'He retired. Not exactly graciously but not exactly broke, either, after I'd pulled things together.'

'And your mother?'

'She departed this life a few years ago in an alcohol-induced haze, which was the only way she could cope with him.'

Arizona gazed at his profile, which was like a rock, and shivered.

He turned to her. 'Cold?'

'No...yes...I don't know.' But she was cold inside, she knew, at this glimpse of the cold, hard core of Declan Holmes, and it crossed her mind to wonder what chance she ever had or would have of fighting him and beating him.

'What does that mean?' he queried quietly.

That I'm attracted to you and scared of you and still mystified by you, she thought, but did not say because it was not her nature to confess things like that, but more, because some intuition warned her it would be fatal. *Why?* she wondered, dazed. *I don't understand* ...

'How about a little warmth, then, of the mutual variety,' he said very quietly and drew her into his arms, but he did no more, and for an age she stood in the circle of his arms trembling then quieting as things, strangely, turned full circle, and it was a bit like being sheltered by a rock ...

She closed her eyes and told herself that just for a moment she would rest and be reassured. It wasn't much longer before he lowered his head and sought her lips, and she breathed anxiously, but he lifted a hand and stroked the smooth skin of her throat down to the satiny hollows at the base of it with two fingers, lightly, until she calmed. Then he claimed her lips again, and she allowed herself to be drawn into a deep, intimate kiss before he broke it gently, held her closer and started to kiss her again.

If anyone had told her, she thought once, that she could be kissed for as long as Declan did it, she wouldn't have believed them, but it was also the feel of him against her, the strength of his legs against her thighs, the long muscles of his back beneath his jacket where her hands now were ... His hands on her hips, slipping under her top and exploring her back, her slender waist, the twin mounds of her breasts, then withdrawing to stroke the nape of her neck beneath her hair. Until finally they stopped kissing and she laid her head on his shoulder, breathing deeply and shakily and feeling an unknown sensation at the pit of her stomach, an intimation of a kind of pleasure that might bind her to Declan Holmes so that she could never break free. And a warning bell struck in her brain....

She lifted her head and swallowed. 'Is that thanks enough?' But she sounded husky and unsure.

He narrowed his eyes. 'It wasn't thanks I had in mind, Arizona. Rather a celebration of our pact.'

'Well—' she licked her lips '—enough celebration then?'

'What do you think?' His voice was dry.

Her eyes widened. 'I...I—' But she couldn't go on, and patches of heat rose up her throat because she knew what he meant.

'You think we should leave that until our wedding night?' he supplied with a sardonically raised eyebrow. 'Is that what you're trying to say?'

'No—well, yes. I...it hadn't actually occurred to me until a few moments ago—I mean,' she said desperately, 'that you, that... Oh hell,' she said hollowly, 'sorry, I'm carrying on like a—child, probably. Sorry,' she repeated, but drew away.

He let her go and she turned away and hugged herself as she stared disbelievingly over the sea.

'A child, Arizona?'

'What do you mean?'

'You said, carrying on like a child, but I wondered if you meant—something else?'

'No.' She said it quietly but quite definitely.

Declan walked round her, took her chin in his hands and tilted her head so that he could look steadily into her eyes. But he didn't tell her what he saw, nor could she read it in his eyes, then he let her go but reached for her hand.

'What now?' she asked nervously.

'Home. And bed. Alone. I think we might have achieved enough for one day, don't you?'

Arizona didn't reply. But she lay in bed, alone, that night and wondered what had been achieved.

She awoke with images in her mind of how pliant and vibrant her body had been in his arms, and the sight, before her eyes, of his arm in a dark blue jacket sleeve over a paler blue shirt bearing a plain gold cufflink carved with the initials DH, putting a cup of tea on her bedside table.

She stared at the dark hairs on the back of his hand wondering if she was dreaming then said groggily, 'It's not Saturday, is it?' I mean—' she bit her lip, confused '—have you taken over from Cloris or something?'

He straightened and she followed the movement with her eyes until they met his. He was shaved, she saw, his hair was brushed and he wore a green and blue tie with his suit. 'No. But an urgent fax was waiting for me when we got home last night. I have to go up to town for a few days. I thought you might appreciate hearing it from me rather than Cloris. It's only—' he glanced at his watch '—six o'clock again.'

Arizona sat up, rubbed her face then pushed her hair back. 'Oh.'

'I could be gone for a week—will you be all right?'

She blinked. 'Of course.'

'I thought you might say that,' he murmured with a faint smile twisting his lips and walked over to open her curtains. She saw then, after adjusting to the light, that he'd brought a cup of tea for himself. It was on her dressing table. 'I meant—' he turned back and picked up his cup '—you'll have Ben to cope with for a few more weeks until the end of this term, you'll still be housebound with Daisy for a day or two, you'll still be at the twins' beck and call—are your nerves up to it, Arizona?'

'Yes,' she said steadily then grimaced as her hair slipped forward and added, before she could stop herself, 'I wish you wouldn't keep catching me like this. Could you pass me my brush and that scrunchie on the dressing table?'

He paused and looked her over before reaching for her brush and the brightly coloured elasticised ribbon. 'I've told you before, you always look—delectable.'

'Thanks,' she said dryly as he handed them over and started to brush her hair with vigorous strokes then holding it in a swathe over one shoulder so she could brush the ends before, with a sigh of relief, she slipped the scrunchie on to hold it at her nape. 'That's better, but you don't have to pay me extravagant compliments.'

He said nothing but sat down in a green velvet armchair and finished his tea. He kept his eyes on her, though, on her watermark white silk, tailored pyjamas with a narrow maroon piping, until finally with a wryly raised eyebrow, he remarked, 'I see you've given away the teddy bears.'

'I haven't,' she replied but with a tinge of colour creeping into her cheeks. 'The kids gave me that nightshirt for my birthday so I wear it as often as possible, but I can't wear it all the time.'

'No,' he agreed. 'Now that's devotion.'

'Not really, it's comfortable.' She turned away and picked up her tea.

'I have a suggestion to make, Arizona.'

'Regarding my nightwear?' she retorted before she stopped to think.

He smiled. 'Well, that, too, eventually, or rather, regarding the *not* wearing of it, but not, naturally, until we're married.'

'Definitely not.'

They stared at each other, Arizona with hostility in her eyes, he with amusement. He also said, 'I didn't come here to fight you this morning, my dear.'

'Then don't bait me,' she replied. 'What did you come to suggest?'

'That at the end of the week, you come up to town for a couple of days. You can stay in a hotel before you get your hackles up any further.'

'I . . . why?'

'So that we can arrange our nuptials. You might like to shop, you might even be interested to see where I live,' he said with irony.

'The children—'

'I appreciate and share your concern for the children, Arizona, but I've made some arrangements that I think might be in *their* best interests while we sort out a few of our own.'

'What do you mean?' she queried after a suspicious pause.

'Rosemary will be delighted to take them and Cloris for the time you're away.'

Arizona stared at him. 'When did you organize this?'

'Last night. I'll also, before I leave this morning, speak to the kids and let them know what's happening—I don't think you'll have a problem. Amongst other things, Rosemary told me that although she's never been able to have kids, she adores them, she will delight in laying on all sorts of fun for them, she's quite certain you need a bit of a break—and if Daisy does get distraught, she'll get straight in touch. It is only a couple of hours drive away. It's less, as a matter of fact, since I decided to invest in a helicopter.'

'You what?'

'Bought a helicopter, Arizona,' he said with a sort of mocking patience. 'I told you I flew them in the Navy.'

'So you did,' Arizona said, a little dazed.

'As a matter of fact it's coming to pick me up this morning— I could have you picked up on Friday if you like.'

'No,' she said hastily. 'If I come I'll drive.'

His eyes told her what he thought of that, but instead of taking issue with it, he said, 'Getting back to the kids, you must know I would never suggest anything that I thought would harm them. But this way they'll be with someone they know, in familiar territory and having fun.'

'Rosemary *is* really good with them,' Arizona said grudgingly.

'Then you'll come?'

Arizona put her cup down carefully and lay back against the pillows. 'Why not?' she said eventually and added, barely audibly, 'As you so often say to me.'

'I did have another thought.' He got up abruptly.

'Oh?'

'Yes, that we get it over and done with at the same time.'

'You mean—get getting married over and done with?' Arizona asked after a long pause.

'Why not?' he parodied with a mocking glint in his blue eyes, and something more, a hint of steel.

'I think I might let you know how I feel about that, Declan,' she said coolly but angrily, 'but I wouldn't hold your breath.'

'All the same, I'd come prepared if I were you, Arizona,' he countered.

'I don't even know where to come!' she protested, and immediately hated herself for such a feeble protest.

He took a card out of his inner jacket pocket and laid it on the dressing table, next to, as it happened, the little crystal bowl that held his engagement ring. 'Check into the Hilton on Friday, I'll make a reservation for you. Give me a call when you arrive and we'll take things from there. Don't,' he warned coolly, 'even think of not coming, Arizona, because I shouldn't be at all amused if you do.' He strode out, closing the door audibly behind him.

I really made him angry, Arizona thought, as she stared, transfixed, at the door. *Did I bring this on myself by being—obstructive? He can't seriously believe I'd marry him like that...*

She looked away at last and felt a curious prickling of her skin as it struck her that perhaps she did wield some power over Declan Holmes, but the kind of power she had no desire to wield over any man....

CHAPTER FIVE

'AH, MRS. Adams, I'm Mr. Holmes's secretary. How do you do? Did you have a good trip up?' a cultured, well-modulated female voice asked down the telephone line.

'Yes, it was fine, thanks,' Arizona replied. 'Is—'

'I'm afraid Mr. Holmes is in a conference, but he asked me to let you know that he'll meet you at the hotel, in your suite, at six-thirty this evening. Did you get the packet when you checked in, Mrs. Adams?'

Arizona glanced at the contents of the packet she'd been presented with by the ultra-attentive Hilton receptionist and closed her eyes briefly. 'Yes, I did. Thank you.'

'Well, if there's anything you need at all, please do give me a call, Mrs. Adams. I made a list for you of the appropriate shops in the area you might like to patronize, and of course, may I offer you my congratulations and very best wishes, Mrs. Adams. Mr. Holmes was kind enough to take me into his confidence, although I gather he wants the wedding to be very private, but you can rely on me to be most discreet....'

Arizona put the phone down moments later, clenched her teeth and thought, *All right, if this is how he wants it, this is how he'll get it,* and she glared at the contents of the packet spread across the desk. A gold Mastercard in the name of Arizona Holmes, five hundred dollars in cash, his secretary's list of the most suitable places to shop for a trousseau and the briefest note from Declan himself to the effect that they would be married at noon the following day.

'I'm so angry I can't see straight,' Arizona said to herself. 'I came up here to try to defuse things, I suppose, and because I've got no choice, anyway, but this kind of treatment deserves—worse! So be it....'

And she shovelled the card and the cash into her purse, left the list of shops on the desk and stalked out of the suite.

Four hours later, she returned, accompanied by a bellboy and a lot of stylish carrier bags. She tipped the bellboy generously, so generously that he bowed out of the suite backwards, and she sat down abruptly, buried her head in her hands and wondered miserably if she hadn't walked right into Declan Holmes's trap.

You should never do things when you're furiously angry, Arizona, she told herself, *you should know that by now!*

She laid her head back with a sigh and thought, *But it's done now so I guess I'll have to live with it,* and glanced at her watch to see that she had an hour and a half before he came, and got up to run herself a bath.

She soaked for half an hour and felt some of her spirit returning. So she opened all her purchases and laid them out on the huge double bed, quite artistically, she thought. Then she dressed, did her hair and made up her face carefully, tidied up and was walking to the lounge when, on the dot of six-thirty, the bell rang. She took a deep breath and went to open the door.

'Arizona,' Declan Holmes murmured by way of greeting, his eyes still the cold, hard blue she remembered from their last encounter in her bedroom at Scawfell, and walked past her into the suite.

She closed the door and after a brief hesitation followed him, saying nothing. And it was like two implacable enemies that they eyed each other across the lounge when he stopped and turned to her.

Until he drawled, as his gaze roamed up and down her, 'Well, well, Arizona—new?'

She looked at the beautiful black cocktail dress she wore, then raised her eyes proudly to his. 'New from the skin out, Declan.'

'I have to say I approve.' The dress had a Thai silk short fitted skirt and strapless bodice, and the gossamer cobweb lace overblouse that tied at her waist had a stand-up collar and puffed sleeves. It was unrelieved black, and the skin of her shoulders gleamed through the exquisite lace, as did her legs, clad in the sheerest black nylons. Her medium-heel suede shoes had pearls embroidered on the heels. Her hair was loose and smooth to her shoulders.

'I'm so glad,' she answered sweetly, 'because there's a lot more for you to approve of. Would you care to take a look?' She held out her hand towards the bedroom.

His lips twisted, but he inclined his head and gestured for her to lead the way. Nor did he say anything immediately once there but scanned the bed and the armchairs all draped with clothes. There was a sensuous collection of underwear and nightwear, silk and lace in gleaming white, French blue, black and one long slim nightgown with tiny straps in a deep ruby. There were several casual outfits, shorts or slacks and jackets or blouses, two pairs of colourful leggings with fabulous printed polyester overdresses. There was a chic linen suit in the palest violet with a grey silk blouse, a long crushed velvet skirt in a colour that reminded one of blue steel with a sheer, fine metal mesh T-shirt to go with it—and beside most of the outfits, a pair of shoes or a handbag, beside some a scarf for her hair or a piece of costume jewellery, a lovely raffia hat or a pair of sunglasses. It was a dazzling collection.

'What do you think?' she asked at last when he'd said nothing for what seemed like an inordinately long time.

'I'm impressed,' he drawled turning to her at last. 'And you did it all in an afternoon, Arizona!' he marvelled. He added, 'Did you take my secretary's kind advice?'

'I did it in four hours, Declan. Just imagine what I could do in a lifetime.' She raised her eyebrows ingenuously at him. 'And no, I did not. I don't need anyone's help to buy clothes, but particularly not your secretary's.'

'So it would seem,' he murmured. 'The one thing I can't seem to find is anything resembling a wedding dress.'

'You're right, there isn't anything that's especially a wedding dress,' she said tautly as his blue gaze, which was suddenly lazy, gave her the oddest feeling of a paralysed prey about to be captured, but she soldiered on. 'For one thing, you probably need a bit more time to choose something like that, and for another, if it's going to be such a rushed wedding, why bother?' She stressed the *if*.

'Well, you certainly have made your statement, Arizona.' But he stopped as she turned away suddenly from his now horribly mocking, insolent eyes, and a visible shudder went through her.

'What now?' he said.

'I'm kicking myself, if you must know,' she said through her teeth.

'Care to tell me why?'

'Because I did all that in a blaze of anger.' She gestured vaguely towards the clothes. 'Because I feel cheap and...I don't know what. Because I walked right into the trap I suspect you laid for me, Declan, *that's* why, but the one thing I don't regret is the lack of a wedding dress.' She turned back, and her eyes were grey and haunted but curiously stubborn.

'You know what's wrong with us, don't you, Arizona?' he said after an age during which she could have cut the atmosphere between them with a knife.

'Yes, probably every last syllable of it,' she retorted.

'Tell me then.'

'I've told you so many times, *surely* I don't have to go through it all again.'

'I don't think we're talking about the same thing at all,' he said dryly. 'Particularly as it's the one thing you refuse to talk about—the mutual hunger that's making our lives quite tormented, Arizona. I don't think you would be making extravagant and hostile gestures otherwise—why bother? And I know I—' he paused '—am getting impatient and frustrated, particularly when I remember how you kissed me.'

'Well then,' she said with an effort, 'why don't I slip into something more comfortable? So we can get this...momentous event over and done with.' She walked past him to pick up the ruby nightgown. 'How about this—'

'Stop it, Arizona,' he said curtly and caught her wrist. 'Anyone would think it was fright motivating you.'

'Oh, but it is, Declan, you scare me and mystify me, but don't imagine I won't overcome it some-how—' She broke off suddenly, her eyes widening as she realized what she'd confessed. 'I mean—'

'You little fool,' he said roughly. 'I'm not going to hurt you.' He gathered her wrists in one hand and drew her right up to him. 'If you stopped fighting me for a while I'd be able to prove that to you.'

Arizona tilted her head so she could look straight into his eyes and said intensely, 'It doesn't seem *right*.'

'Well, what would you like?' he countered. 'That we declare undying love for each other? I thought that kind of thing was anathema to you.' His hand ground into her wrists and she sagged suddenly against him. He released her immediately but caught her around the waist, saying after a long moment, 'Just give up, Arizona.'

'I'm not that kind of person,' she whispered.

'Why don't you wait and see what kind of person emerges? You might get a surprise.'

She closed her eyes, frustrated, and flinched as he started to kiss her eyelids, but he ignored it and con-tinued to kiss her until she shivered, but this time un-deniably with pleasure.

She stirred about half an hour later, and laid her head on Declan's shoulder with a little sigh.

'All right?' he asked quietly.

'Yes...'

They were in the lounge with only one lamp on and the fabulous lights of Sydney stretching down to the harbour below them from the Hilton tower. She was in his arms, sitting on his lap, with her legs stretched along the settee, her shoes on the floor beside them and, temporarily at least, all the fight in her smothered beneath a tide of exquisite sensuality, evoked and aroused by his hands and lips. What was worse, she thought, was that this was only a brief respite because he was leading them down a path from which there was no return and she didn't, couldn't care.

It was doubly ironic when he said very quietly, 'Do you want to go on—or stop?'

'Don't . . . stop,' she murmured and added with absolute honesty, 'I don't think I could bear it.'

He traced the outline of her lips and watched the sudden wariness that came to her eyes. He'd discarded his jacket and tie, and she could see the springing black hairs where his shirt was opened. She resisted an almost overwhelming temptation, as she waited and wondered what his response would be, to touch them.

He said at last, 'You look as if you're expecting me to crow with triumph.'

'Do you want to?'

He laid his head back and fiddled with her hair with the hand that was around her shoulders while his other one lay possessively on her waist. 'I can't deny a certain feeling of that kind—' he smiled a ghost of a smile '—but for the most part I'm almost overwhelmed with relief.'

Arizona moved and he looked into her widened eyes. 'I've wanted you for over two years, Arizona,' he said quietly. 'That's a long time. Will you come to bed with me now?'

'Yes.'

'I forgot,' she said huskily as they surveyed the bed, still strewn with her purchases.

'If you take one half, I'll take the other,' he said with a grin and let go of her hand. It only took them five minutes to clear the bed, and he pulled off the cover, but it was long enough for Arizona to be attacked by guilt and a sudden sense of shyness, so that when he held out his hand to her again, she hesitated.

He watched her briefly then came round to her side of the bed. 'You could return them all tomorrow and we could start again, from scratch,' he said gravely.

She grimaced and coloured faintly. 'I made them cut all the price tags off.'

'Did you now—were you that angry?'

'Yes,' she whispered.

'Then will you accept my apologies for doing that to you?'

'Declan—'

'No—' he put a finger to her lips '—let's just concentrate on this—have you any idea how lovely you are? Should we examine that aspect of it and the effect it's had on me?' he said wryly.

'What do you mean?' she said uncertainly.

'Sit down and I'll tell you.'

So she sat on the bed after a moment's thought, and he sat beside her, close although not touching her. 'I think it all started with your eyes,' he mused. 'So clear and piercing at times, then so totally noncommittal at others or—worse. Such as the day, I think it was the second time we met, that you looked across the lounge at Scawfell at me and virtually told me with your eyes to do my damnedest. I can even remember what you wore, a black blouse and a long skirt that rustled as you walked. I can remember cursing that skirt, in fact, because it hid your legs. I still have the same problem whenever you wear anything long.' Arizona couldn't help smiling faintly.

He took her hand in his but did no more. 'Then there was your temperament,' he went on, surprising her. 'You were so positive in everything you said or did, so constructive. You also, even in your governess days, got around, when I was there at least, as if I was of absolutely no consequence, as if I was quite beneath you and always would be. I admired that,' he said but added with a wicked glint as he looked into her eyes, 'when it didn't invoke a sense of—we'll see about that, Arizona—in me. So what have we got now, your eyes, your temperament—ah, yes,' he murmured, 'your body. Now that was quite another matter,' he said and said it so soberly she frowned.

But he went on in quite a different, much lighter tone before she could say anything. 'So you see, I've rather been like the beggar at the feast all this time. And that's why I haven't always been—quite rational, and that's why having you sit here next to me with the perfume of your skin and hair tantalizing me, the thought of taking your beautiful dress off you all but driving me crazy, not to mention the thought that you might have changed your mind—all those things are particularly hard to bear,' he finished gravely.

'You...I...don't know whether to believe you,' Arizona said with another smile curving her lips.

'Believe me, lady!' he replied laconically.

'But I didn't know you could be like this,' she persisted, although she was still smiling.

'No?' He raised a rueful eyebrow at her. 'Well, you have sometimes given me the impression you imagine I'm the grab-them-by-the-hair-and-yank-them-into-your-cave kind of man. I must say you do look at me with just that kind of suspicion in your eyes, Arizona,' he said reproachfully.

'Sorry,' she murmured, and the part of her that was incurably honest made her add, 'I just didn't expect this, though.'

'Well, I hope it's been a nice surprise—if not, I could always go back to being a strong silent type if you like. I did tell you,' he said suddenly with no amusement, 'that you might not know what you were fighting so dedicatedly.'

'I know. The thing is,' she said slowly because she was in fact thinking deeply, 'I've never seen you with a woman before, one of your own, I mean.' She grimaced awkwardly but continued. 'You never brought anyone like that to Scawfell, did you? So—' she'd been studying her hand in his but she glanced at him now '—perhaps that's why I didn't know what to expect, but there must have been ... women in your life.'

'Some,' he agreed.

'None that you wanted to marry?'

He paused and considered. 'When I was twenty-two I was madly in love with a very voluptuous blonde, and I can recall being quite desperate to marry her—for the space of about three weeks.'

'Seriously,' she said quietly.

'Seriously, Arizona?' He lifted a wry eyebrow at her then said soberly, 'Yes, I've thought about it once or twice before, once particularly, a few years back.'

'Will you tell me who she was? I mean, what she was like and why—you didn't.'

'She was—' he paused and looked straight ahead with his eyes narrowed '—a very well-known businesswoman, very independent, very intelligent. There was no way,' he said deliberately, 'despite what we felt for each other, that we could live together, as we discovered to our mutual cost. It's been over for nearly five years now.'

'Was she younger or...?'

He looked at her. 'A couple of years younger—why do you ask?'

'I was wondering whether she had the maturity or whatever it takes not to be sort of flattened by you,' Arizona murmured.

Declan grinned and glanced pointedly at the array of clothes around the room.

'That's different. You goaded me into doing that,' Arizona protested.

'I did apologize,' he reminded her and added, 'should we try to stick to the lighter side of things, though? I actually made you smile a couple of times earlier.'

Arizona flinched.

'What's that supposed to mean?' he said softly.

'I feel ridiculous now, that's all. As if I'm making heavy weather of things for no good reason.' She shrugged a touch desolately.

'On the contrary, when you were kissing me, things were electrifying. Should we try that again? But could I make a request first?'

'What?'

'This beautiful lace blouse—is it a separate entity?'

She frowned. 'From the dress, do you mean?'

'Uh-huh. Because if it is, I thought we might take it off. I'm dying to get closer to your skin.'

Arizona hesitated then undid it at the waist and he helped her to slip it off. 'Mmm,' he murmured, sliding his hands down her arms, 'that's what I meant. How about the dress?'

She tensed, then forced herself to relax. 'It unzips down the back.'

But he made no move to reach the zip. He took her in his arms instead, saying, 'On the other hand, why hurry?'

'Why, indeed,' she murmured, somewhat dazed.

But it was only a few minutes later, during which time he'd merely stroked her skin while she'd laid her head against his chest and listened to the beat of his heart, that she reached behind her and pulled down the zip herself.

She also said huskily as he tilted her chin and looked enquiringly into her eyes, 'I'm being positive, I guess. As I used to be once. I'd sort of forgotten that.'

He kissed her lips. 'I'm delighted.'

She smiled a wry little smile. 'The only thing is— I don't quite know where to go from here.'

'Could I take over then?'

'If you would, Mr. Holmes...'

She woke to a total feeling of disorientation. Then it started to come back to her and she groped across the bed but she was alone, so she pulled a pillow into her arms then realized a shaft of light was coming from the bathroom, and a dark shadow was standing in the doorway.

She blinked several times, adjusting to the gloom, and saw that it was Declan with a towel tied around his waist, his shoulders propped against the doorframe as he watched her. Then he straightened, turned on an overhead light and came over to sit on the bed.

They said nothing for a long moment, just stared at each other, and Arizona drank in the way his wet hair fell over his forehead, the still damp skin of his shoulders and chest, and remembered the feel of his body on hers, the strength of it and the way he'd held her and made love to her until she'd felt as if she was spinning off the planet like a singing top as she experienced the first climax of her life. Remembered how stunned she'd been afterwards, lost for words, incredulous—and helpless. For that matter how she felt now, only a couple of hours later, but all the same as if she might never leave this bed, but not only because she was tired—because she really felt like luxuriating between the sheets and feeling as if he was still there with her.

Then she thought she should say *something*, so she murmured huskily, 'You're dynamite, Declan.' But her eyes were completely serious as she added very quietly, 'Thanks.'

He smiled faintly and cupped her cheek. 'Don't thank me, Arizona. You had the same effect on me.' He paused and narrowed his eyes as he added, 'It didn't seem to me as if it had ever happened for you quite like that before.'

'No,' she said after the slightest hesitation.

'How do you feel about it?'

'Like...Alice? In wonderland?' she suggested after a moment. 'I seem to remember reacting a bit like that.'

'You reacted wonderfully, you were exquisite. It's just a pity I have to leave you,' he said slowly and took her hand.

She tightened her fingers around his and said with a frown, 'Why?'

'I have an urgent meeting this evening—I know, it seems a strange time for business but it affects what goes into tomorrow's paper. There's a political crisis looming about which we have to be very careful what we say. Besides, it's supposed to be unlucky for prospective brides and grooms to spend the night before their wedding together, or something like that.'

Arizona grimaced. 'So they say—will we still be doing it tomorrow?'

His eyes locked with hers. 'Oh, yes. Did you doubt it after what's just happened?'

'No...'

The door chimes rang.

She tensed and her eyes widened.

'Stay there,' he murmured. 'I ordered some food, I'll get it.' He disappeared into the bathroom, came out wearing a towelling robe and walked into the lounge. A few minutes later he reappeared pushing a trolley with the most visible things on it being a silver bucket with a bottle of champagne—and a bouquet of red roses. 'For you,' he said and put the cellophane-wrapped flowers into her arms. 'And for us.' He picked up the frosted bottle.

Arizona stared at the perfect red blooms and was curiously touched. 'I've started a rose garden at

Scawfell, I love roses. Thank you.' She lifted her eyes to his and they were suddenly wet.

'Here,' he said softly and put a glass of champagne into her hand. 'Drink it. It will help.'

It did. So that when he removed the flowers she was able to ask him to pass her the ruby nightgown and her brush and once she'd slipped into the nightgown, she sat up and brushed her hair, rearranged the pillows behind her and smiled at him ruefully. 'Sorry, I don't often get emotional.'

'If you think I mind making you a bit emotional, I don't at all. What would you like? There are oysters or fresh prawns, there's smoked salmon, a couple of slices of hot quiche and a salad—I didn't think you'd feel like a huge meal so I ordered a bit of this and that,' he said humorously.

'I would love some smoked salmon then some quiche.'

'Done, I'm yours to command!' And he served her food then drew a chair up beside the bed for himself. And they ate companionably, talking desultorily and sipping champagne.

Until Arizona lay back with a sigh of contentment. 'I feel wonderful,' she said, a bit surprised.

'Tell me,' he murmured with a wicked little glint in his blue eyes.

'Well, I feel as if I could go back to sleep, a beautiful sound sleep.'

'Good,' he commented. 'Because much as I regret this, I have to leave shortly.' And he got up, stacked the trolley, poured her the last of the champagne and started to dress.

Arizona watched him and knew that he'd organized things so she would feel this way, but a little part of her mind wondered if he knew that above all, she would still fall asleep preferring not to be on her own for the rest of the night.

Nor was it a help, as she sipped champagne, to have to watch him dressing economically and methodically, to watch him buttoning up his blue shirt and remembering how wide his shoulders were and how they'd felt beneath her hands, how she'd twined her fingers gently in the springy dark hair of his chest . . .

He came back to the bed with his tie in his hand. 'About tomorrow—would you trust me to take care of it all?'

'What do you mean?' she said after a moment.

'Well, I'd rather you didn't leave the hotel, or indeed the suite, until I send a car for you.'

Her eyes widened.

'Only—' he paused '—because if anyone gets wind of this they're liable to hound you to death.'

'The media, do you mean?'

'Uh-huh. So, say I send a car at ten-thirty?'

'And all I'll have to do is bring myself? And my new clothes?'

'Yes.'

'I . . .' She hesitated, dazed. 'I suppose so.'

'You could relax,' he suggested with a suddenly crooked little grin.

'Do I look as if I need to?'

'You look—' his gaze travelled down the beautiful nightgown and back again to faint blue shadows beneath her eyes '—utterly lovely.'

She closed her eyes suddenly and said, 'Don't go.' Then her lashes swept up and there was a faintly horrified expression in her eyes. 'I mean . . .'

'Arizona, I have to,' he said evenly. 'I'm sorry. But nothing will tear me away tomorrow, after noon.'

She blinked, then smiled. 'Okay. Sorry. I'm fine really. And I won't so much as venture outside the door.'

'Good girl.' He stood up and dropped a light kiss on her hair. 'I'm also only a phone call away, you know. Why don't you ring Rosemary, incidentally?'

'I'd already rung Rosemary twice before you came,' she said wryly. 'They're all fine. But—' She stopped and frowned.

'Glory be!' He tied his tie and slipped his jacket on and she saw him do a check of his pockets and all of a sudden he was Declan Holmes again, media magnate, not the man who had lain beside her with his strong, beautifully proportioned body naked and who had made stunning love to her.

And to distract herself, she said, 'So! Until noon tomorrow.'

'Until noon, Arizona.' And their gazes locked and it was as if by some mysterious force, she was in his arms again, helpless with pleasure... And after what seemed like an age, he turned away and walked out.

She woke the next morning with the children on her mind, but each time she reached for the phone something held her back. She was still undecided and worried about them by nine o'clock when her doorbell chimed. It was a bellboy with a suitcase and a note for her.

She took them, somewhat dazed, and opened the note first. It was from Declan and it said simply, 'The rest of my night was as lonely as hell. Don't wear the dress until you get to the house, you'll be able to change there. P.S. I chose it myself.'

She turned to the suitcase and opened it with unsteady hands. There was a dress box inside, and from the tissue paper within she drew a dream of a dress. It was in a pearl-coloured delicate crepe with a three-tiered slim skirt, a sleeveless round-necked bodice and a short jacket embroidered with tiny seed pearls to form little flowers. Just the elegance and grace of the outfit as well as the beautiful workmanship caused her lips to curve into a smile, and she held the dress to her cheek for a moment. Then she noticed two smaller parcels in the case, which turned out to be a pair of kid shoes that matched the dress and the much smaller one, another velvet box from which she drew, with a gasp, a river of flawless pearls with a ruby clasp.

The house turned out to be a two-storied mansion on Point Piper above the harbour with a fabulous view. A housekeeper met her as the car drew up and showed her to a bedroom that was obviously the master bedroom with French doors that opened on to a veranda, and another note from Declan to the effect that the ceremony would be in the garden and he would meet her there at noon. In the meantime, she was to do as she liked and ask for whatever she wanted.

Arizona asked the housekeeper for some tea, which came in a silver pot with some macaroons, and sat down as the door closed behind the polite housekeeper with a sigh and a feeling, definitely this time, of Alice in Wonderland.

And to distract herself, she looked around then got up to inspect the lovely bedroom. It had a velvety, close-pile pewter blue carpet, a king-size bed covered with a quilted ivory silk spread with a trim that matched the pillowcases in shadowy hyacinth pinks and greys. The windows were dressed similarly, ivory silk curtains with hyacinth and grey pelmets and tie backs. There was a breakfast table and two chairs set at one window and two deep armchairs set in front of a fireplace. The walls were papered in a thick matt slate blue with an ivory trim, and there were crystal and silver ornaments on the mantelpiece and occasional tables dotted about. There was also a full-size dressing room leading off the bedroom and into an ensuite bathroom, a symphony of blue and silver. She lingered in the dressing room, touching one of Declan's suits almost as if she could imbibe some of his spirit to give her courage. Then she looked at her watch and realized she only had three-quarters of an hour before she became Mrs. Declan Holmes. And was touched by a moment of panic, unreality and the feeling that she shouldn't be doing this without having warned the children it was happening. She returned to her dress, laid out across the bed, and fingered her engagement ring, and there was a soft knock on the door, which revealed the housekeeper again but not only that, Sarah, Daisy, Rosemary and Cloris.

'Oh!' Arizona gazed at them for a moment, taking in the girls' new lovely matching blue silk dresses, Cloris in matronly mauve, Rosemary in a stunning green décolleté outfit, and then they were all kissing and hugging each other, Arizona with some tears of happiness in her eyes.

'It was Declan's idea,' Daisy told her, sitting on the bed while the others helped Arizona to dress. 'He said he wanted it to be a surprise for you.'

'We all flew up in his new helicopter!' Sarah contributed enthusiastically. 'Do you think the boys aren't wrapped in it?'

'They're here, too?'

'Sure are, but Declan reckons the boys stay together and out of the girls' way on wedding days. You should see them. They've got new suits just like proper men!'

'And where did all these lovely new clothes come from?'

'That was my doing, darling,' Rosemary said, not without a certain smug air as she urged Arizona to sit down so she could attend to her hair. 'Got a call from Declan yesterday morning asking me if I could rustle up the goods, so I rang David Jones with all the details, and they came down on the helicopter this morning.'

'And I brought these,' Cloris said proudly. She opened her purse and withdrew two handkerchiefs, a beautiful old handmade-linen and crochet-trimmed one with tiny blue forget-me-nots embroidered in the corners and an obviously new one trimmed with lace. 'You know what they say, something old, something new, something borrowed, something blue? Well, this belonged to my mother and I'll lend it to you for today, so it's old, it's borrowed, it's got some blue and the other—'

'You're an absolute darling,' Arizona said huskily and hugged her.

'How was that?'

Arizona looked at the new gold wedding band on her left hand and up into Declan Holmes's eyes and was curiously speechless. They were alone for the moment in a small latticework gazebo where they'd

been married by a marriage celebrant in a simple ceremony with the children, Rosemary and Cloris as wit-
nesses. It was a clear, sparkling day, and the waters
of Sydney Harbour were like pale blue stretched silk.
The gazebo was beautifully decorated with flowers and
ribbons, and the white wrought-iron table they'd stood
before had been clothed with an exquisite linen cloth
embroidered with silver thread. The celebrant, an elegant woman in her fifties, had spoken quietly but
wisely on the joys and pitfalls of married life, calling
on some of her own experiences as a wife of twenty-
five years and the mother of four children with touches
of humour. Arizona, during the ceremony, had found
herself more moved than she'd expected to be, more
relaxed with the children about them obviously feeling
happy, excited and important.

'It was,' she said, 'fine. You're an excellent or-
ganizer, Declan.' She looked around and added genuinely, 'It's all lovely. Thank you so much for bringing
them up. I was—worried about doing it behind their
backs.'

'So was I. It didn't feel right. They don't seem to
have any problems with it, do they?'

'No.'

'And how does it feel to be my wife?' he murmured
with a slight smile quirking his lips.

'I'll have to let you know about that. It's only been
ten minutes.'

'Do you think ten minutes is long enough for me
to kiss you? Properly, that is.'

Arizona hesitated and looked towards the house
through the latticework.

'We're alone,' he said, following her gaze.

'I know, but they—'

'There's a feast set out up there. I doubt we'll be interrupted for a minute or two.'

'In that case, you may,' Arizona said.

CHAPTER SIX

THEIR wedding feast was laid out in a lovely long veranda room with huge glass windows facing the view. There was a table for eight set with silver and crystal, decorated with flowers and ribbons—and if the bride looked a little bemused it was because she had just been very comprehensively kissed. The bridegroom, however, looked completely at home, and it was a gay meal as they ate asparagus vinaigrette, roast turkey with pine nut stuffing and Cointreau ice-cream. And after it, he made a little speech to the effect that he was 'borrowing' Arizona for a short honeymoon right here in Sydney, but that they'd both be back at Scawfell in a few days, and in the meantime Rosemary and Cloris had a few surprises planned for good children.

Daisy looked vaguely mutinous for a moment, but when she discovered they were to fly back in the helicopter, she brightened immediately. It seemed she'd taken to it like a duck to water, although Sarah did say in an aside to Arizona that she'd probably be unbearable at school boasting about it. But it was a happy, contented band they waved off a little later.

Then Declan led her inside, saying wryly, 'Alone at last—I hope you liked my choice of a dress. As soon as I saw it I could visualize you in it, looking unapproachably lovely.'

Arizona blinked then glanced at her outfit. 'I love it, but it doesn't seem to have made me unapproachable.'

'Yes, it did,' he contradicted. 'For the first few minutes when we met in the gazebo, you were just that.'

'Well,' she confessed with a faint smile, 'that's because I really felt like Alice in Wonderland. Why—' she hesitated '—did you want me to look unapproachable?'

'A purely masculine whim. I wanted to contrast that in my mind with how you might look later. Sit down,' he invited and poured two glasses of champagne. They were in the room overlooking the harbour, but the remains of the feast had been magically cleared. He took his glass and said gravely, 'May I toast the bride?'

'Thank you,' Arizona responded. 'May I toast— us?' she added very quietly.

'With great pleasure, my dear.' They clinked their glasses together and stared into each other's eyes. Then he dropped a light kiss on her hair. 'Do you know, we're absolutely alone now.'

'Oh?'

'Mmm—I gave the staff some time off. I thought you might prefer it that way. For a while.'

'Thanks, I would.'

He looked into her eyes then said lightly, 'Would you like a tour of the house?'

'Yes, please.'

So he showed her around and told her a bit of its history. It was grander than Scawfell, filled with beautiful old furniture and paintings, and in one of the most prestigious suburbs of Sydney, the view alone guaranteeing that, but what surprised her was that he'd bought it for his mother.

'Why?' she asked as they got back to the veranda room.

He shrugged. 'I thought she deserved something like this. She didn't have long to enjoy it, unfortunately.'

'And your father?'

'He moved out after she died. In fact he moved out of the country. He lives in London now.'

'Does he know about us?'

Declan looked at her. 'No.'

'Wouldn't he approve?'

'I've no idea. Does your mother know about us, Arizona?'

'I wrote to her this morning.'

'Will *she* approve?'

'I don't know.'

He went to say something then seemed to change his mind. She looked at him enquiringly.

'It just occurred to me I was in no position to lecture you on parental relationships—what would you like to do now?' he asked, changing the subject completely.

Arizona hesitated then was unable to stop herself from yawning, but he only laughed as she grimaced. And said, 'Why not? After a meal like that it's entirely sensible.'

'What about you?'

'I'm going to join you—but only for a nap at this stage,' he said gravely. 'It is my wedding day, too, you know.'

'Well, that's what I wondered,' she said honestly.

'Whether I was going to leap on you straight away?'

'Yes—no...Declan, you're teasing me. But I didn't think you were the napping type, nor that you would have been consumed by nerves this morning.'

'Ah, but I was, of a kind,' he said. 'You could have run away.'

Arizona's eyes widened, and he smiled slightly then said simply, 'Come.'

She changed out of her wedding dress in the privacy of the ensuite dressing room and put on a long T-shirt, and she fell asleep in his arms and slept deeply and dreamlessly for nearly an hour. By which time long shadows were stretching across the garden and the pool. But she was alone when she woke, and after a few moments of reorientating herself, she got up and padded over to the window where she saw him, sitting beside the pool in bathers with a mobile phone on the table beside him, reading through what looked like a pile of documents. She grimaced then searched through her new clothes for the swimsuit she'd bought, plain white and one-piece, but low-cut at the top and high-cut at the legs.

And she grimaced again as she eyed herself in the mirror. It was deliberately sexy, this swimsuit, and clung to her figure like a second skin. There was a white voile shirt that went with it, but it was so sheer it didn't hide much, either. She put it on all the same, tied her hair back, and with an odd little breath, went to join her husband.

He wasn't there when she got to the pool, although the phone was. She shrugged and looked around. The pool was in a walled garden with flowering creepers growing riotously over the mellow, old pink bricks. There was thick smooth grass on three sides of it then a paved area that led out of a side veranda and some dark green garden furniture. There were small statues dotted about that were also plant holders with flowering shrubs growing out of them. There was a bower, smothered in climbing roses, and a small waterfall at one end of the pool. It was a lovely, peaceful, scented and very private area.

She took her blouse off and was just testing the water with her toes when she heard a low whistle. She straightened and turned to see Declan with a tray in his hands, walking towards her.

'Oh. I wondered where you were,' she said a little breathlessly.

'I went to see where you were and to bring us some drinks,' he replied, putting the tray down without taking his eyes off her. 'We must have just missed each other.'

'The water looks so inviting.'

'So do you. That costume is quite stunning.'

Arizona laughed a little then said ruefully, 'It's not exactly my usual style.'

'No? So it was one of your heat-of-the-moment purchases? Designed to teach me a thing or two, one way or another?'

'Yes, but I'm not sure what,' she replied.

'In that mood, perhaps an eat your heart out, Mr. Holmes type of message?' he suggested with the wickedest glint in his blue eyes.

Arizona blushed but couldn't deny it. 'Perhaps.'

'Thank God things have turned out the way they have, then,' he murmured wryly. 'I'd be an absolute case, otherwise. Would you like a swim first or a drink first?' He gestured to the tray. 'It's not alcoholic, just very cold and refreshing fruit juice.'

'I think I'll have a swim first.' And so saying, Arizona dived into the water. It was heavenly, also refreshing, and she swam quite a few laps energetically before she pulled herself out and accepted the dark green towel he handed her.

'Feel better?'

'A whole heap better!' She rubbed herself down and wrung out her hair. 'Thanks,' she added, sinking into a chair.

'I—hell,' he said as the phone rang. 'Sorry about this, but it will be the last one today, I promise.'

It was a fairly long conversation, and she couldn't help divining it was to do with the current political crisis, something she'd normally have been very interested in. She grimaced as she thought that nothing outside her immediate situation seemed to have the power to interest her or hold her attention, and as she sipped her drink her mind wandered to the night before, what had happened and how it had happened—and when it was likely to happen again. So that it was out of quite a considerable reverie he brought her when he said her name.

She coloured faintly because she hadn't even realized his phone call had ended. 'I was miles away.'

'Where, I wonder?' he murmured.

She coloured more brightly this time but said honestly, 'I was thinking of last night.'

'So have I been, all day—could this be the right time to relive last night?'

'I don't know. I mean—' her lips twisted into a wry little smile and her eyes were suddenly mischievous '—we could wait until we go to bed tonight.'

'That might be harder than you think,' he responded.

'But...' She hesitated and looked at her hands then shrugged. 'I don't know how to begin, I guess.'

'May I make a suggestion?'

She grinned. 'You always do, and, much as it has pained me on occasions, they're nearly always good ones.'

'Thank you! That might even spur me to greater heights. Let's see. Had you noticed that the sun has just set?'

'Uh-huh.' Arizona looked around. The garden was now a mysterious place of rose-tinted shadows, and the sky was reflected on the pool in streaks of orange and lemon amidst the glassy blue surface of the water. 'I've also noticed,' she said impishly, 'that you never rush into your suggestions. You often set the scene first, so to speak.'

He raised a wry eyebrow at her. 'Any guesses?'

'No—well, only a very general idea.'

'Good. I like surprising you. Uh—the air is warm and balmy, would you also agree?'

Arizona eyed him through her lashes. 'Yes.'

'How was the water?'

'Lovely,' she said slowly.

'Ever swum without your clothes?'

A little jolt of breath escaped, but she took time to say thoughtfully, 'As a matter of fact, no.'

He sat forward and picked up her hand. 'Would you like to try it?'

Arizona felt a tremor run through her and, foolishly, looked around and up at the sky.

'They'd need a helicopter,' he said amusedly. 'I assure you, no-one would see, other than me.'

'All right.' But she bit her lip, then on an impulse, freed her hand, stood up, stripped her costume off and dived into the pool. When she surfaced, though, he was right beside her and he was laughing at her, his teeth glinting whitely, his dark hair plastered to his head, and he resisted the sudden rush of embarrassment that made her try to twist away by gathering her slim, satiny body in his arms and holding her against the length of his as he trod water then moved them to a shallower area where he could stand. 'Don't,' he said as she made another effort.

'Don't laugh at me, then,' she retorted.

'If you knew what I'd really like to do to you,' he replied, 'you'd know it was no laughing matter at all. But,' he continued, overriding her, 'don't you like this?'

Arizona quietened suddenly and thought about it. Or felt it, would have been more to the point, she reflected, and in the sudden gesture of freedom it seemed to generate she wound her legs around his thighs and lay back against the circle of his arms, murmuring, 'I hope this speaks for itself!'

'It does,' he agreed, his gaze intent on the water lapping around her breasts, the chill of which but not only that had caused her nipples to unfold and stand erect. 'Most eloquently, my lovely mermaid. Did you know you were a symphony of rose and ivory and the most tantalizing curves?' His hands moved down to her buttocks, and she floated on her back, still with her legs twined round him and a dreamy sense of delight in her heart. But he hadn't finished, it seemed. 'Then there's this lovely slender waist—' he moved his hands upwards, and her skin felt slippery and satiny '—and a veil of darkness here.'

She gasped and shuddered as he traced his fingertips through the mound of curls that guarded the core of her most secret, sensitive area.

'No good?' he said, barely audibly.

'Too good,' she whispered, and pulled herself upright, slipped her arms around him and laid her cheek on his shoulder, her breasts against his chest. 'If you see what I mean,' she added with a tremor in her voice. 'Is it any good for you?'

'So good, my dear,' he answered, 'I'm going to get you out of here before it's ... too late.'

'Not very far away, I hope.'

'No...'

In fact he carried her out of the pool and laid her on the grass beside it and it felt wonderful beneath her, thick and cool, and he knelt over her for a while, running his hands up and down her body, tasting her skin and her nipples while she stroked his back and moved with ever growing desire until she said his name urgently, and he parted her legs and claimed her powerfully and equally urgently so that they were united in a burst of white-hot passionate delight.

'How... does it always happen like this?' Arizona said shakily, many minutes later but still cradled in his arms.

'There's certainly something about us that's—highly combustible,' he said. 'How do you feel?'

She considered and moved against him for reassurance, warmth and the pure pleasure that the grace and strength of his body brought her. 'I feel ... very womanly,' she said at last.

'Do you mind?' he asked quizzically.

'Right now, no. I love it. But if you'd ever asked me whether I would enjoy making love on a lawn beside a pool in the dark, I think I might have been quite scornful,' she confessed.

He kissed her hair lightly and grinned. 'Then I'm honoured, Mrs. Holmes, to be the one to bring you to this state. Talking of the dark, though, and the possibility of getting chilled, would it be terribly mundane if I suggested we should go inside, have a shower and put some clothes on?'

'No, as usual, Mr. Holmes, it's an excellent suggestion!'

They showered together, and it was while she was drying her rose and ivory body with a huge, snowy white towel before a wall of mirrors, and studying it quite openly and with some curiosity, that she was struck by a sudden thought.

She turned to Declan, who was towelling himself off also, and said, 'Is that what you meant?'

He raised an eyebrow at her, hung up his towel and came to take hers from her. 'Meant?'

'I mean—did you plan that all in advance?' Her eyes were very grey and serious.

'I planned to make love to you some time today,' he said gravely and put his hands on her waist. 'But, no, I did not say to myself, we'll do it by the pool at six-thirty on the dot after an unclothed interlude in the pool. Why do you ask?'

'What I really meant was, when you said earlier that you wanted me to look unapproachable so you could contrast in your mind—' She stopped abruptly.

'Ah, that,' he drawled. 'Yes, the contrast is quite stunning.' And his blue gaze swept up and down her body, from the top of her head to the tips of her toes and all the flushed, silken, curved and slender spots in between. 'Does it bother you?'

'No,' Arizona said slowly, but it did. For no reason she could put her finger on, though.

He narrowed his eyes. 'You don't sound too sure.'

She moved, but he kept his hands on her waist. Then he surprised her—he turned her around so they were both facing the mirror, she standing in front of him, he looking at her inscrutably.

'What?' she whispered after a long, tense moment.

His eyes met hers in the mirror and he brought his hands up and cupped her breasts. 'It's mutual, Arizona. We do this to each other, don't we?'

'I . . . yes,' she said uncertainly then closed her eyes and laid her head back against him as those long fingers plucked her nipples almost absently. 'But again? I mean . . . so soon?' Her voice cracked a little.

'We've a bit of lost time to make up for,' he said, rather dryly she thought, but before she could take issue, he added, 'I'm afraid it can't be soon enough for me at the moment.' And without waiting for her permission, he picked her up and took her to the vast bed in the master bedroom. But what surprised her most, perhaps, was the corresponding hunger he was able to arouse in her, again, so soon and despite her better judgment for another, obscure reason.

But there was no doubting that he did arouse her, and as their limbs mingled and his hands sought and stroked and teased, her breathing grew ragged and she stretched her arms above her head and pointed her toes and made an odd little sound in her throat as she grew warm and wet, and ached for him to commit the final act. Which she participated in with growing boldness that secretly amazed her but seemed only to please him until they were breathing as one and the pleasure ran through them at the same moment.

Minutes later, he rolled onto his side, taking her with him in his arms, and said into her hair with a tinge of amusement, 'For a second time, and so soon, how was that?'

'It was—I can't actually describe it,' she whispered. 'But I do know I'll be good for absolutely nothing for a while. You've worn me out, Mr. Holmes, although I must say you did it beautifully.'

He laughed and hugged her. 'Go to sleep then.'

And she did.

She woke alone, saw drowsily on the bedside clock that it was ten o'clock at night, and for a few minutes simply lay with her hands at her sides wondering where he was. Wondering if millionaires had separate bedrooms. Wondering if it was common amongst them to spend the first night of their marriages in separate beds and rooms. Then she realized she was hungry and thirsty, and she shook off her odd feeling of foreboding, had a quick shower, pulled on the dark blue towelling robe that hung behind the door and padded to the kitchen.

The light was on and Declan was there in shorts and a T-shirt with a percolator of coffee bubbling aromatically on the gleaming range. The kitchen was tidy but the remains of their turkey was on a platter on the table. He looked up as she stood in the doorway and simply held out his hand.

Arizona hesitated then slipped into a chair beside him. 'I wondered where you were,' she said quietly.

'I was starving but I didn't want to wake you. Like some?'

'Yes, please.' She looked around.

He carved her some cold turkey and buttered her some bread. 'Coffee?' She nodded and he got up to pour it.

'So you're fairly domesticated,' she reflected between mouthfuls of turkey.

He glanced at her quizzically. 'Well, the Navy teaches one all sorts of useful things. How to open a tin of baked beans, for example.'

'Seriously,' Arizona said.

'Seriously?' He raised a wry eyebrow at her. 'Did you have me pictured as some dangerous beast you might have to house-train?'

'No, of course not.' Arizona grimaced. 'I just don't know, well, those kind of things about you. Some men are great cooks. Pete was, for example.' She stopped abruptly.

Their eyes met, and she tingled curiously, not only because as soon as she'd said it she'd wished fervently she hadn't mentioned Pete's name, but also because of the sudden little glint of steel she thought she saw in the blue depths of his eyes.

'I know,' he said at last. 'No, I'm not in Pete's class cooking-wise, although I mightn't starve if left to my own devices. How did you cope with Pete's uninspiring lovemaking, incidentally?'

Arizona went cold and her eyes widened. 'What do you mean?' she said with difficulty.

'Did you fake it?' he suggested.

'No.'

'He must have wondered what he was doing wrong.'

'He knew . . . he—' She pushed her plate away suddenly and stood up. 'Why are you asking me this, Declan?'

'You brought his name up, Arizona,' he said with irony.

'I'm sorry about that,' she said evenly. 'It just—' she paused '—came out in the context of what we were talking about. It wasn't because I'd been thinking of him or anything like that.'

'How kind of you,' he said dryly and put two mugs of coffee on the table. 'Going somewhere?' he added coolly.

'I . . . it crossed my mind to wonder whether the honeymoon was over,' she said tautly. 'If so, I might as well go back to bed, alone.'

'Sit down, Arizona,' he ordered. 'Let's not get all dramatic.'

'You started this,' she countered.

'Perhaps I have an unusual sensitivity on the subject. It is, after all, our wedding night.'

Arizona stared at him because the way he'd said it didn't seem to match up with what he'd said. In fact there'd been a flat sort of indifference in his voice that made her blood run cold and made it very hard for her to believe that she'd genuinely touched a nerve even though she knew it was not in the best taste, if nothing else, to mention one's previous husband to one's very new husband.

'Is—' her voice shook slightly 'something else wrong, Declan?'

'Such as?' He raised an eyebrow at her.

'I don't know. I'm only guessing. Perhaps I didn't altogether please you last time round.'

'Not at all, Arizona,' he drawled. 'You please me exceedingly. But *you* were the one who came into this room with something on your mind, then brought Pete up.'

It was true, of course, only she'd forgotten that in the last few minutes. But it struck her suddenly, so that she bit her lip as the words formulated in her mind—*yes, I always seem to wake up alone and it bothers me!* But the implication of that sentiment suddenly hit her with a force that made her close her eyes briefly and then sit down as she swallowed unexpectedly. *Have I fallen that much in love?* she wondered.

'Arizona?'

She swallowed again then lifted her coffee mug. 'Not really—I mean there wasn't much on my mind. I—'

The telephone rang.

Declan swore then lifted the wall receiver, and his voice was hard as he said hello. But it was Rosemary, worried because Daisy kept waking up with nightmares and asking for Arizona.

'You better talk to her,' Declan said and handed her the phone.

She got Rosemary first, who said, 'Darling, the last thing I wanted to do was interrupt your honeymoon but she seems quite upset and I just can't get her to stay asleep. None of us can! I think she might have had just a bit too much excitement today.'

'Let me say hello, Rosemary.' And a moment later, 'Daisy, is that you, pet?'

'Arizona,' Daisy wept down the line, 'I don't want to stay here any more. I want to go home and I want to see you and I can't sleep because there's cars smashing and crashing and—'

'Daisy.' Arizona tried to stem the flow. 'Darling, I'm coming home first thing in the morning, I promise you! Now I'll tell you what I want you to do. You know your Christopher Robin book? Well, get it out and let Cloris read it to you, it's your favourite book, remember? Tell you what, why don't I say some of it to you now?'

'But I've got the book here.'

'I know it off by heart, we both do, don't we?' Arizona said gently. 'So what shall we start with? You choose...'

Fifteen minutes later she put the phone down and rubbed her brow wearily, feeling drained and tense.

Declan watched her for a moment then walked over to her, put his hands on her shoulders and started to massage them. He also said with a strange little smile, 'I can see we are going to be hard put to get much more of a honeymoon. It was probably my fault— too big a day today.' He grimaced. 'But I did want them to be here for you—for their sakes and yours.'

Arizona searched his eyes but that steely glint was gone. So was the indifference, but at the same time his blue gaze was entirely enigmatic. She moistened her lips and thought that she'd never felt more at sea with Declan Holmes than she did now. 'I know, and I'm grateful, but I did say I'd go back tomorrow...'

'I heard. Does she get these nightmares often?'

'Not for ages.' His long fingers were working a minor miracle.

'It's just going to take a bit more time, I guess. You look exhausted. Come back to bed.' And he released her to take her hand. *Just like that,* she thought, dazed, as she went with him obediently. *Did I imagine the rest?*

And she stood compliantly while he slipped the blue robe off and slid the ruby nightgown on over her head.

'Did you leave the teddies behind?'

She blinked. 'Oh—yes.'

He smiled. 'I'm glad in a way. You look about nineteen in it. Certainly not both a wife and a widow. Hop in,' he invited and pulled the bedclothes back.

But Arizona stared at him, her eyes dark and shadowed, and seemed unable to move. So he picked her up and laid her down as if she was a child, then he got in beside her, turned her on her side so she was facing away from him and took her in his arms.

She moved once, but he slid his hand slowly down her flank and said into her hair, 'Go to sleep, Arizona. It's been a big day all round.'

She did, after a while, thinking that it might have been too big a day for her as well as Daisy, because she didn't seem to understand anything any more, and certainly not why she should be falling under the soothing spell of what this man was doing to her, a man who was her husband but in some respects a complete stranger. Nor why he should be doing it after the things he'd said.

And she woke in the morning with the same thoughts on her mind, and reached across the bed suddenly—but she was alone.

CHAPTER SEVEN

'WELL, I won't go looking for him this time.'

Her words seemed to echo and she sighed, laid her cheek on the pillow and wondered if she was being childish or ridiculous or particularly fanciful. *But for some reason it does make me uneasy,* she mused, *and it probably was just that uneasiness that led me into committing the solecism of mentioning Pete on our wedding night, although it wasn't really such a solecism, did he but know it . . .*

The thing is, she thought, *I've got the oddest feeling that he expects it to be all or nothing for me, which doesn't quite fit in with our mutual concept of this marriage and might not be what I'll get from him. Then again, the real thing is, does the fact that always waking up alone upsets me mean I'm going to want more than I'm going to get from Declan Holmes? And if that's the case, I'm in trouble . . .*

She stared unseeingly across the room then closed her eyes briefly. Five minutes later she got up and started to pack. Then she showered and dressed in a shorts suit outfit made from silky crepe in thyme green with a tiny beige dot, a beige blouse to go beneath the jacket and thyme flat shoes. It was one of her purchases and was cool, elegant and uncrushable for travelling.

She was just closing her last case when the door opened and Declan came in with a tray.

126

'Ah,' he murmured after one long moment when they stared at each other, 'you're up. I was hoping to bring you breakfast in bed.'

'Thank you. But I'm up, as you see,' she replied evenly.

'And still annoyed with me.' He crossed over to the table by the window, put the tray down and pulled out one of the chairs with a polite gesture. He added with a wry lift of an eyebrow, 'Why don't you sit down and tell me all about it?'

Oh, no, you don't! Arizona thought, and sat down, composed. 'I didn't say that, Declan.'

'Everything points to it, however.' He sat down opposite, removed some covers and revealed two perfect herb omelettes. There was also fresh orange juice and toast.

'I don't see why,' she answered calmly. 'This is a fair jump from opening a can of baked beans,' she added quizzically.

'Would that it were—the staff are back.'

'I see.' Arizona said and refrained from saying, *so the honeymoon is over.* He was also dressed, in a grey and white striped shirt, maroon tie and charcoal trousers.

'Well, I guess as soon as I've finished this I can head for home.' She paused. 'The only thing is that my car is still at the Hilton, but perhaps you wouldn't mind giving me a lift into town? I gather you won't be coming down with me.'

'As it happens, I'm going to give you a lift to Scawfell, although I won't be able to stay,' he said and continued to eat his omelette imperturbably.

'You don't have to drive all that way, Declan, I'll be fine.'

'I'm sure you will,' he murmured, 'but I'm not driving you, I'm flying you.'

'And how will I get my car back?' Arizona enquired.

'I'll have someone return it for you. It may interest you to know that one of the reasons I acquired a helicopter, apart from not wasting my Navy training and because I do have to hop about the place such a lot, was that I thought it would bring me back to your side much more quickly than any other means.' He caught and held her gaze and raised his orange juice to her.

'Ah, but I imagine it will do the opposite just as speedily,' Arizona commented with considerable irony.

His blue gaze hardened and he put the glass down. 'My dear, I don't know if you have any idea what the country is going through at the moment or how peculiarly it affects my business—'

'I do, I do,' Arizona interrupted. 'I realize all sorts of things. That Daisy is waiting anxiously, for another, that this is how we decided our marriage would be— I'm not complaining, Declan.' She glanced at her packed bags, at her purse and sunglasses set neatly ready and waiting on the bed. 'I'm being if anything most cooperative, I would have thought,' she finished gently.

'At the same time as you'd like to scratch my eyes out,' he said after a tense little pause.

Arizona sipped some juice and slipped the stem of the glass between her fingers before she said dryly, 'Dear me, Declan, do you really think I'd be so uncouth?'

'Not uncouth at all,' he corrected her as dryly. 'But I really think that were we to go to bed now, you'd fight me every inch of the way, and enjoy every minute of it.'

Arizona stood up and slammed her knife and fork together beside her unfinished omelette. 'Don't count on it, and don't dare to lay even a finger on me,' she warned him furiously.

'Sit down, Arizona,' he recommended, not angrily nor even particularly coldly, but something in his eyes warned her to obey him or suffer the consequences.

She tightened her mouth and sat down.

He waited a moment then said evenly, 'What are we fighting about, Arizona? If it's still to do with you being forced to marry me, let me ask you this. Do you regret sleeping with me at the Hilton, do you regret me making love to you beside the pool or here in this very bed? If you do I have to tell you you're a sensational actress. Do you regret being able to go back to Scawfell and starting to do all the things you've been wanting to do for ages?'

'I . . .' She clenched her fists in her lap. 'No.'

'So?' He gazed at her narrowly.

'I think you better take me back to Scawfell, Declan,' she said very quietly. 'It's just possible that new brides are a bit emotionally unstable,' she added and wondered if he knew the effort it cost her to smile slightly. 'Sorry.'

'In that case I think there's something else I ought to do.'

Her lips parted as she suddenly recognized the way he was looking at her. And she trembled inwardly.

'But only to—warm and reassure you,' he said. 'Not fight you.'

'You really don't have to, Declan,' she said, barely audibly. 'I'm all right.' *And I now know exactly what I'm up against,* she thought, but again, did not say.

'On the other hand, would you like me to?' he asked.

'Like you to?' She hesitated.

'Make love to you.'

She stared at him helplessly.

They landed on the lawn in front of the house a couple of hours later, and everyone was there to meet them, Cloris, the children and Rosemary.

'I'm so, so sorry,' Rosemary whispered to Arizona, but Declan immediately took charge of things as he picked Daisy up and hugged her then handed her to Arizona, saying, 'If anyone's interested in a joy flight over the ocean I've got a bit of time.'

He didn't have to make a second offer. Richard and Ben raced for the machine, as well as Sarah, although Daisy elected to stay with Arizona. And Rosemary urged those staying on the ground inside, saying she had a surprise, which took the form of a wedding present.

'Oh, Rosemary!' Arizona gasped.

'Like it?'

'It's stunning!'

It was, in fact, a full-size, black-faced, woolly, extremely lifelike sheep. 'Not that easy to choose gifts for the very wealthy,' Rosemary said wryly, 'but it's beautifully made by a little man who lives down the coast, and his work is starting to be highly sought. I'll leave it up to you to find a spot for it,' she added with a lurking grin.

'Thanks, pal.' Arizona kissed her warmly. 'I think he's beautiful. Why don't we put him in the hall? Then he can greet everyone who comes to Scawfell. Daisy, darling, would you like to think of a name for him?'

Daisy brightened and let go of Arizona's hand for the first time. 'Bendigo,' she said promptly. 'Can I have a ride on him?'

'Bendigo,' Rosemary and Arizona said together, and laughed.

'Couldn't have done better myself,' Rosemary remarked.

A little later, Cloris waylaid Arizona as she came in alone from farewelling Rosemary. Declan had been duly introduced to Bendigo then dragged off to the stables by the kids. And once Cloris had said again that she was so happy for Arizona, how right it all was, and so sorry she hadn't been able to calm Daisy down the night before, she asked Arizona which bedroom she'd like her to prepare.

Arizona frowned. 'I don't understand—anyway, Declan can't stay tonight.'

'I know, but Mr. Holmes told me that you—you and he—that is—' Cloris blushed '—would be using a different bedroom. He brought down a bag of clothes and things and I just wondered where to put them.'

'Oh, I see! Just leave them where they are for the time being, Cloris, until I have a moment to think about it,' Arizona said brightly but feeling foolish underneath and thinking, *Why does he do this to me?*

She was in her own bedroom when he came back from the stables, starting to unpack. He closed the door, looked at her profile then came over, wrested the bundle of clothes from her hands and took her in his arms. 'Remember me?' he queried quietly.

'Declan—'

'The man you slept with this morning?' he persisted.

'Declan, of course—'

'And the way it was?'

She quietened abruptly in his arms and felt a tide of colour creep up her throat. 'Yes,' she said huskily, and laid her brow on his shoulder as she was shaken by the most intimate memories.

'But you're angry with me again.' He said it as a statement, not a question.

She breathed in the heady masculine essence that went to make up Declan Holmes, felt the strength and hardness of his body even through his suit and said a little wearily, 'No. I'm not.'

'Arizona.'

She raised her head and looked into his eyes and knew she would have to come up with some explanation because he could read her too well. 'Cloris told me you wanted us to share another room.'

He swore beneath his breath but said straightly, 'Yes, I do. I didn't expect her to tell you, though.'

Arizona smiled sketchily. 'I thought you might have known Cloris better than that by now.'

He grimaced. 'I will from now on. But I thought that that's at least what you would want to do yourself—'

'Declan,' she interrupted, 'Pete and I never used this room. It was to be my—retreat, and that's what it was.'

He frowned faintly, and she could see the ramifications of what she'd said going through his mind.

She opened her mouth to add something, but a wariness that not even their magnificent lovemaking of that morning could altogether dispel made her stop and bite her lip.

'Then there's no problem, is there, Arizona?' he said slowly. 'So why are you upset?'

'Because I can't help wondering whether the shadow of Pete isn't going to hang over us all the time.'

He searched her eyes intently. 'Because *I* didn't want to use a bedroom you and he had used? I would have thought that was perfectly natural—'

'Because it was his house, because—' She broke off. 'Do you really think I would have done that to you?'

'I'll tell you what I think,' he murmured after a moment and cupped her face gently. 'That we're at cross-purposes for no good reason at the moment. Tell me something, would you mind me sharing your retreat with you?'

'Oh...no.'

'Then that's resolved that,' he said and kissed her.

And she stood in the circle of his arms for a while longer until he took her hand and said, 'I have to go. Coming to see me off?'

'Yes. But not because I want to.'

'I'll be back as soon as I can, I promise you.'

'Thanks.'

'So, tell me all about married life,' Rosemary said chattily on the veranda at Scawfell a fortnight later over a cup of coffee. The children were at school— Ben at his new school now—and Cloris could be heard humming in the kitchen. The old house drowsed in the sunlight and bees hummed in the flowerbeds below the veranda. The sea was an inky blue, and you could hear the surf below the cliff. Rosemary had called in on her way back from the village.

Declan had been home four times in the past fortnight, but only for a night each time.

'Married life?' Arizona said, and added unguardedly, 'well, we certainly don't live in each other's pockets.'

Rosemary said after a moment, 'He's a very busy man, no doubt. It's just a pity, I expect, that the kids depend so much on you, but that could improve.'

'Oh, I don't mind.' Arizona recognized as soon as the words left her lips that she was trying to backpedal, and a glance at Rosemary revealed that she, too, thought the same.

Damn, Arizona thought. *Well, there's only one thing to do and that's soldier on.* 'I mean I don't really think I'm cut out to be a tycoon's wife, and I'd just as soon be here instead of jet-setting around the place.'

'Besides which,' Rosemary said energetically, 'when you get to be married as long as I have, you don't want to be living in each other's pockets. How is Daisy?'

'She's fine. In fact they're all benefiting from Declan even though he's not here such a lot. But he seems to leave a presence behind him, of law and order—' she grimaced '—and growing confidence that their lives aren't going to be torn apart again.'

'There you are then!' Rosemary looked triumphant. 'Before long you might be able to go on a delayed honeymoon. I was really so sorry I couldn't calm Daisy that night, your wedding night of all nights, but she was just inconsolable, absolutely distraught. You know, Arizona,' she continued thoughtfully, 'I don't think any of us realized what you've had to cope with or just how marvellous you've been, and I have to tell you, with my famed delicacy, that a lot of us thought Pete might be doing the wrong thing when he married you.'

'Thanks,' Arizona said with irony.

'Don't hate me, darling.'

'Rosemary, I don't,' Arizona said with a cross between a grin and a sigh.

'Are you in love with Declan?'

'Now, Rosemary, your famed delicacy has gone a little too far—'

'It's just that it's a bit hard to tell with you, my pet.'

Arizona paused, considered then said barely audibly, 'A little too much perhaps.'

'Do you think you can ever be too much in love with a man... who is also your husband?' Rosemary queried after a long pause.

'Yes, I'm afraid I do, but look—' Arizona smiled with genuine humour then '—I'm probably a bit strange in these respects. Rosemary, seeing as you're so well-named, would you like to see my rose garden? Declan sent me down *twenty* new varieties the other day.'

Indeed, she thought as she worked in her rose garden that afternoon, Declan, who might only grace her bed from time to time, was certainly providing her with plenty to think about and plenty to do. Not only twenty new rosebushes to plant and plan for but plans for a glass-roofed conservatory to be added to the house, which he'd thought they might be able to use as a summer dining room as well and in which, he'd said, she could grow all sorts of exotic plants. It had

been impossible to hide the quickening of interest this
had aroused in her. He'd also taken her up on a chance
remark that the cliff path down to the beach was a
bit dangerous and sent a team of workmen down to
cut some steps out and erect a handrail. And he'd
asked her if she'd like the inside of the house re-
painted, and when she'd agreed that it did need it,
had left the choosing of colour schemes, if she wanted
to change anything, up to her. Added to this he'd insisted on hiring a gardener for her, to do all the heavy
work and help her to implement all the ideas she had,
and to occupy a vacant cottage in the grounds. A man
who didn't seem to have much feel for growing things,
she thought once, but did have a passion for neatness
and order and was extremely self-effacing. With the
net result that the estate of Scawfell was starting to
look its best.

Whereas I, she thought as she sat back on her heels,
*feel as if I'm in a state of limbo, despite having all
this to do and think about, not to mention Christmas,
not that far away, to plan for. Why can't I just be
happy, or if not that, content? Because every minute
I'm away from Declan Holmes is extraordinarily hard
to bear,* she answered herself. *If only I hadn't been
so righteous, so sure I couldn't fall in love like this.
How did it happen to me so quickly and completely?
Is it the sex? This passionate attraction that I might
even be confusing with love? Am I more like my
mother than I ever dreamt possible?*

Strangely enough, she got a letter from her mother
the next morning, in reply to her letter telling her she
was getting married.

'Dear Arizona,' she read. 'Your news came as a bit of a shock. I had hoped that by now you would have forgiven me enough for all I put you through to have confided in me earlier about this second marriage, but I do hope with all my heart that you'll be happy, darling. Is it a love match? You didn't say so, in fact you said so little I don't know what to think and all I can tell you is that you're in my heart and my prayers constantly. Yes, I had heard of Declan Holmes, although not lately....'

Arizona stopped reading because tears were blurring her vision and she whispered, 'Oh, Mum...'

She took the kids for a swim about a week later on a Thursday, a week or so during which she'd seen nothing of Declan. It was a searingly hot day, and the surf was delicious. But it was a tiring exercise nevertheless because Daisy was still a very novice swimmer, and even Sarah and Richard had to be watched all the time in the waves. They, however, were still full of energy after their swim and they bounded up the now safe cliff path and disappeared from view while she was still gathering together towels.

And knowing they could come to no harm, she lingered a little, slipping her togs off beneath her towel and putting her button-through dress on, then discarding the towel, shaking them all then simply standing staring out to sea with the bundle in her arms. Until she began to get hot again and with a strange little shrug turned towards the path. Declan was waiting for her at the top. Declan, casually dressed in jeans and a sports shirt, looking big, fit and entirely enigmatic.

She gasped and grabbed the handrail. 'I didn't hear the helicopter! I didn't expect you . . . how long have you been here?'

He took his time answering as his blue gaze roamed over her, her wayward damp hair blowing about her face, her pretty floral dress with a heart-shaped neckline and its line of buttons down the front, her bare legs and feet and said finally, 'I drove. I've been *here* for the last few minutes.'

'Why didn't you come down?' she asked and wondered why she sounded, and felt, nervous.

'You looked oddly deep in thought.'

'I . . .' She stopped and grimaced.

'You also look tired,' he added and took the towels from her.

'I'm fine! Did you see the kids?'

'Yes. I've given them a treat.'

'Such as?'

'Cloris is taking them into town for a movie and then a hamburger dinner.'

'Declan!' she protested. 'It's a school night.'

'I can guarantee that once every Pancake Day, it won't hurt them.'

'I suppose not,' she said ruefully. 'It will be nice and peaceful for a while.'

'That's also what I thought,' he murmured and took her hand.

But he didn't seem to have any more to say to her, and they walked up to the house in silence, although hand in hand, and he simply dropped the towels on the kitchen floor and led her upstairs to the cool green bedroom where he not only closed the door but locked it.

'Just in case they come back early,' he said and crossed the carpet to stand in front of her. 'May I?' He looked at the top button of her dress then into her eyes. Arizona started and coloured.

'What?' he queried quietly.

'I've just remembered I've got nothing on underneath,' she said self-consciously and wondered what she could have been thinking of on the beach.

'I know.'

'How?'

'I saw you change very modestly beneath your towel. There was no evidence of any underclothes, but I really don't think it matters at this point. Do you, Arizona?'

She grimaced. 'No. All the same, it was an odd thing to have done.'

'As I mentioned, you did look oddly preoccupied.' And there was a query in his blue eyes.

She coloured again but said, 'There's a lot to think about at the moment. The conservatory, the new colour schemes, the garden, Christmas—all those things.'

'I wondered if you were missing me.' He put out a hand and touched the top button then slipped it free of the buttonhole.

Arizona looked down as his fingers moved to the next button and it met the same fate. 'Well, yes,' she tried to say lightly. 'It's been a while, I guess.' It had in fact been exactly a week and two days, she knew, almost to the hour.

He smiled, but not with his eyes, and she shivered suddenly as the last button gave way and her dress fell open. 'Not too long?' he said, making no move to touch her.

'Declan...' Her voice sounded strangely hoarse. 'Is something wrong?'

'Why do you say that?'

'I don't know. I—don't know.'

'No, nothing that this won't cure,' he said after an age and raised his hands to slide the dress further apart and cup her breasts.

She took an unsteady breath, and he moved his hands down to her waist and the curve of her hips, and the dress slipped off her shoulders so she was exposed, the whole slim, curved, salty length of her. And he studied her body minutely, as if renewing his acquaintance with it, studied the delicate ruffled pink of her areolae, the paler satin of her skin that the sun didn't see, moving his hands again and drawing his fingers very lightly up the curve of her breasts then lingering slowly on a path down to her thighs.

'Declan,' she whispered, trembling finely not only with exquisite pleasure but some strange sense of unease, 'don't...'

'Don't you like it?' he said looking into her eyes but never for a moment ceasing to move those fingers over her skin. She looked away and stood for a moment with her hands clenched into fists at her sides, her head bent, her dress caught only on her upper arms now. Then she raised her eyes to his and said honestly, 'I'd prefer it if I didn't feel like an object somehow.'

'Then why don't you tell me you were thinking of me on the beach, Arizona?'

Her lips parted and her eyes widened and she turned away, or tried to, but she stumbled, and he caught her wrist and steadied her, and brought her right back in front of him where she'd been, saying only with a cool smile chiselling his lips, 'Arizona?'

'All right, if that's what you want to hear, I was,' she answered tautly.

'But not that happily?'

'If you're trying to make me say I missed you, yes, I did,' she replied but tossed her hair in a suddenly defiant gesture.

'And you take exception to that?'

'What would be the point? And I suppose now you're here I might as well make the best of you—is that what you'd also like me to say, Declan?'

'In fact it was something else I had in mind,' he murmured.

She blinked. *'What?'*

'Oh, something along the lines of welcome home,' he drawled. She opened her mouth to say that this was no more home to him than the moon, just a temporary stopping off place where there was a convenient bed and a bedmate, but stopped herself with her eyes darkening as if she'd received a blow because, of course, these conditions were as much her choice as his, or had been . . .

'Welcome home then,' she said in an oddly choked voice and brushed a tear away. 'Sorry. I seem to be making a habit of saying that to you. But I didn't expect you and I suppose I got a bit of a shock.' She swallowed. 'And I didn't think you were particularly welcoming, either, so perhaps we should—both start again?'

He released her wrist and she gathered her dress about her.

He watched her then said only one dry word. 'How?'

She attempted to smile and attempted to be honest. 'If you'd like to take me to bed I think I'd need to be held for a bit and possibly talked to, not for long, just a while. And I think you know,' she said slowly, 'that another habit I've acquired is to respond most favourably to you in bed—that hasn't changed. When—' her voice shook '—I don't feel I'm being... when I'm...' She stopped and swallowed again.

'Being treated as an object,' he supplied. 'That's what you said.'

'Yes, well—yes.'

'It would be strange if we had the same problem, wouldn't it?'

She licked her lips. 'What do you mean?'

'Oh—' he frowned faintly then shrugged. 'One day you might work it out. In the meantime, of course, I'm quite happy to bow to your preferences.' And without warning he picked her up and laid her on the bed, lay down beside her on his stomach with his chin propped on his hands, and said, 'What shall we talk about?'

Arizona sat bolt upright and said through her teeth, 'I could hit you, Declan Holmes!'

'Okay,' he said obligingly and sat up, possessing himself of her fist, 'but let me show you how. Most women go for the good old slap, whereas a punch in the mouth is probably doubly effective and doesn't leave you with a ringing hand. But then again—' he looked into her flashing eyes with the corners of his mouth twisting '—I think I'd rather be kissed.' And he dropped her fist, pulled her into his arms, said into her hair, 'For what it's worth, Arizona, I've missed *you* and I'm sorry I've been gone for so long.'

*   *   *

'Oh . . .'

'I know,' he agreed and buried his head in the curve of her shoulder some time later. 'This certainly hasn't changed.' And she felt his long body shuddering on hers.

'The really strange thing,' Arizona said later when they were lying in each other's arms beneath the sheet, and stopped.

'Go on,' he prompted.

'No. It's rather embarrassing.'

'Look, you have to tell me now,' he said with a crooked grin. 'Or I'll start imagining heaven knows what.'

'Well, it's this,' she said ruefully and couldn't stop herself from running her fingers through the thick dark hair that lay in his eyes. 'I feel incredibly calm.'

He kissed her palm and said, amused, 'It may be strange to you, but I can assure you it's a great boost to my ego.'

'I don't believe that for one moment,' Arizona said, equally amused.

'Then you don't know me as well as you think.'

She was silent for a long time, revelling in being nestled against him, in the calm and serenity that lay on her spirit like a balm, not able to care that this might be a very temporary state.

'How long do you think this will last?'

'This calm or the calm of having no kids pounding around the place?'

'Well, both, I guess.' She looked at him wryly.

He kissed her brow and smoothed some strands of hair from her cheek. '*This* calm for a few days, because I'm staying down over the weekend. Kids calm,

I regret to say, for another hour at the most, but you don't have to get up—'

'Yes, I will. A whole weekend,' she added and bit her lip.

'There's a downside, unfortunately. I have to go to the States for about a fortnight on Monday.'

Arizona was silent then she moved against him and said, 'Never mind.' Her lips twisted mischievously. 'I'll make the most of my weekend.'

'Good girl.' He kissed her again.

If she was delighted to have him for the weekend, so were the kids, and supremely, so was Cloris. The weather held and they swam, rode together, not Cloris, but she was in her element cooking up magnificent meals, and on Sunday she packed a gourmet picnic lunch and they drove to Ben's school, which was having an open day and a gymkhana.

Ben seemed happy and contented and rode Daintry well enough to be presented with a rosette. It was, for Arizona, a happy though different experience—the first time she was introduced, in this case to the headmaster, as Mrs. Declan Holmes, the first time she was out in public as such.

She said to Declan that night when they were alone in the green bedroom getting ready for bed, 'Despite your fears, the press has shown no tendency to hound me. For which I'm duly grateful, but all the same.'

'It's funny you should say that, Arizona.' He raised a wry eyebrow at her. 'Because I was about to mention it to you.'

'Oh?'

'Mmm... It can't remain a secret forever, so I thought it would be a good idea if we gave one interview when I get back, as unrevealing as possible, but enough to satisfy them and not have our marriage seen amidst all sorts of speculation.'

She stirred. She was sitting in bed against the pillows with her knees drawn up, watching him pack, taking pleasure in his economical movements and his brown body in a white T-shirt and shorts. She was wearing her ruby nightgown, her hair was brushed and shining and her beautiful diamond ring shone in the lamplight on her finger. 'Here?' she said.

'No. In Sydney. Nor do I plan to mention Scawfell.'

Arizona twisted her ring.

'They might know about me, anyway.'

'Because of Pete? They probably will, but they'll be working for me, you see.'

'I see.'

'Don't look so concerned, it's the best way, I promise you. I've also upped the security here.'

Arizona blinked. 'It must be very unobtrusive.'

'It is. Did you never suspect—' he grinned at her '—your new gardener?'

'No.'

'Well, now you know. You get on well with him, don't you?'

'Yes, I do,' she said slowly, thinking of the tough, weather-beaten man in his late forties she'd quite come to like. 'But why couldn't you have told me?'

'I didn't want you to feel—hemmed in or whatever. And resent him in consequence. Now that you *do* know, though, he's here to protect your privacy and the kids', as well as your persons and the property. By the way—' he dug down into his bag and brought out a parcel '—I forgot to give you these.'

Arizona, who was frowning anyway, frowned at the parcel he placed in her lap, but didn't open it as she said slowly, 'He must be very versatile.'

'He is. We were in the Navy at the same time, and I had the opportunity to save his life once. He's been rather devoted ever since. He's also been at a bit of a loose end ever since he got out. He's a loner, no wife or kids, so this job, so he tells me, suits him down to the ground.'

'Oh,' She still didn't start to open the parcel.

'What are you thinking?'

She registered the slight change in the tone of his voice and wondered whether to tell him that what she resented was not being taken into his confidence, being treated like a child, in fact, then decided against it. She looked up with a brief smile instead, and said, 'I'm thinking that you're managing my—our—life very competently.' And tore the brown paper to gasp at what she saw. A photo of them on their wedding day in a beautiful silver frame.

'Oh, it's lovely.' She lifted it to the light and studied herself in the dress of his choosing, unsmiling but looking oddly uplifted whilst he was looking at her enigmatically.

'Glad you like it.' He took it from her and put it on the bedside table. 'There's a smaller one, too, which I thought we might give to Cloris.' He lifted the other one out.

'She'll be thrilled,' Arizona said wryly then sobered suddenly. 'Are there any more prints?'

'Yes. Why?' He handed her a photo envelope.

'I thought I might send one to my mother.'

'Have you heard from her?'

'Yes.' She hesitated. 'It occurred to me I should stop—feuding with her.'

'Why not?' he said as he so often did. He added, 'What brought that on?' And sat down on the side of the bed.

Arizona shrugged and avoided looking at him. 'Nothing special, but it's been a long time, and she is my mother, I guess.'

The silence stretched until she was forced to look into his eyes and was slightly disturbed to see the narrow, rather intent look she was on the receiving end of. So she said, 'Will you send one to your father?'

He continued to look at her narrowly for a few moments more then said, 'I hadn't thought of it, no. But why don't you ask your mother to come down and stay for a while?'

'Oh, she wouldn't do that,' Arizona said hastily. 'But this is a start, I guess.'

'I guess,' he repeated. Then he seemed almost deliberately to change tack as he picked up the silver-framed photo again. 'Remember what happened later, on this day?'

Arizona thought of the walled pool garden in Sydney and swallowed unexpectedly. 'Quite accurately, as it happens,' she said huskily.

'Well, I was wondering if you would consider taking your beautiful nightgown off for me now, and while I'm not suggesting we seek a pool or anything like that, we could try to recreate other aspects of that—happening.'

A faint flush rose to her cheeks, but her eyes were grey and steady as they held his, although her voice was not quite steady as she said, 'I would...like to do that, Declan,' And did it.

He remained as still as a statue as her hair sank about her shoulders and the lamplight played on her breasts, then he took her in his arms in an oddly convulsive movement and his voice was curiously unsteady as he said, 'Arizona, I wonder if you know what you really do to me?'

He was up, dressed and ready to go when she woke the next morning but, for once, she didn't care. Because she still had those words on her mind and in her heart, and they seemed to sustain her without his presence beside her to wake up to.

CHAPTER EIGHT

SHE was sustained, a little to her surprise, nearly all of the time he was away, and when she made herself analyse it, she discovered it was because he was out of the country that she didn't seem to mind being alone so much.

So what does that mean? she wondered and decided, after more thought, that it meant she believed there were absences he couldn't avoid, such as this one—and those he probably could in this day and age of fax machines, mobile phones and so on.

The disturbing nature of these thoughts prompted her to resolutely try to banish them from her mind. The other thing that intruded now and then was the idea of going public about their marriage, and she realized that she was uneasy about that.

But his homecoming saw a passionate reunion between them, plus his insistence that she spend a few days in Sydney with him, although he made no mention of an interview. He also decided against relocating the children to Rosemary's, vetoed her idea of taking them to Sydney, as well, and took Daisy for a walk on her own. From which Daisy returned bursting with pride but would not be drawn on the subject.

'What did you say to her?' Arizona asked curiously, later that evening.

'We discussed,' he said with a wry little smile, 'her importance in the scheme of things, how it upset you to know she was unhappy, especially when it was for no real reason—and for good measure I threw in a bribe.'

'Declan?'

'My dear Arizona, look at it as an incentive system, then. Kids thrive on incentives.'

'And just what incentive did you *bribe* Daisy with?' she asked ominously.

'I told her that if she showed us she was grown-up enough to spend a few days with Cloris, without you, I would consider her grown-up enough to start riding lessons on her own pony. I also told her it was our secret, just between the two of us.'

Arizona tried to maintain her expression of severity but failed. And said through her laughter, 'Oh, God, if *that* works I'll—I don't know what I'll do!'

He laughed, too, then said, 'You know that pale violet suit you bought when you were—planning to show me a thing or two?'

'Yes. Why?' Arizona asked ruefully.

'I've never seen you in it.'

'You haven't seen me in a lot of those clothes. But why now? I mean, it's ten o'clock at night.'

'Would you humour me and try it on, though?'

She looked at him him strangely then shrugged. 'Come up in about five minutes.'

Five minutes later she stood in the middle of their bedroom wearing the lovely linen suit with its pale grey blouse and a very high-heeled pair of grey kid shoes.

'Mmm,' he said, walking around her. 'Yes, that will be excellent. You have great taste in clothes, Arizona. Even when you're spitting mad,' he added with a wicked little glint in his eye.

'Thank you,' she replied. 'Would you mind telling me what all this is about, though?'

'I think this will be the perfect outfit to be interviewed in tomorrow, that's all.'

She stilled and eyed him narrowly then said coolly, 'I wish you wouldn't spring these things on me, Declan. I am old enough to be consulted.'

'I told you before I went away that we'd be doing this, Arizona,' he said mildly.

'You may have—you did,' she corrected herself as he looked at her a little mockingly, 'but you've said nothing since you got back, and, well—' she gestured then said exasperatedly '—is that why you want me to come to Sydney?'

'One of the reasons, yes. But it will take an hour of our time, at the most.'

She swung away from him and went to sit by the window. And heard herself say rather desolately, 'I don't want to do it.'

'How would you like to handle it then?' he queried dryly.

'I have no idea. I'd rather it didn't have to be handled at all.'

'Arizona,' he said impatiently, 'this is only a magazine interview—'

'I don't want to be splashed over the pages of a magazine, in my violet suit or out of it—'

'I'm sure you'd cause a sensation out of it, but it's not that kind of magazine.'

'You know what I mean,' she said tautly. 'But I particularly don't want to be parcelled up to look like an appropriate wife for a millionaire or to be seen holding hands with you, looking coy or whatever.'

'How about simply looking as if you're in love with me?'

Some heat rose up her throat, but she said bleakly, 'I'm surprised you want this, Declan, I really am. I thought you valued your privacy.'

'It's exactly because I do value my privacy that I'm doing this, I thought I'd explained that to you. Don't you want people to know we're married, and if so, why?' he asked curtly.

'It's not that,' she answered slowly. 'You've managed to keep it pretty private until now.'

'That's mainly because you've been incarcerated at Scawfell most of the time,' he said impatiently. 'Arizona, trust me on this.'

'All right.' But she said it stonily.

He stared at her bent head and the way her hands were clasped in her lap, then swung on his heel and walked out.

Nor did he share her bed that night, and they drove to Sydney the next morning in a chilly sort of silence for the most part. Until Arizona said abruptly, 'Don't treat me like this, Declan. And all because I expressed some very natural reservations about being exposed to about seventeen million people.'

He glanced at her briefly but long enough for her to see the glint of steel in his blue eyes. 'Nevertheless it's what we'll be doing this morning, my dear.'

'I'm surprised you didn't add something along the lines of—so you might as well make the best of it,' she said contemptuously.

'Those were your words, not mine.'

'On another occasion when I felt I was being taken advantage of. You're right.'

He swore beneath his breath and then, taking her by surprise, pulled the car off the road. They had not reached the outskirts of Sydney, and it was on a grassy verge beside a huge, open paddock that he switched the engine off.

'What are you doing?' she asked evenly.

'I'm going to have this out with you here and now, my beautiful but unreasonably stubborn *wife*.'

'Declan,' she said through her teeth, 'you may call me what you like, but the fact that you were able to force me to marry you should not lead you to imagine I am going to be like putty in your hands!'

'No?' he drawled.

'No,' she snapped back.

'Of course there are times when you're not exactly putty in my hands but—'

'Don't,' she said coldly but with a sudden flush staining her cheeks.

'I suppose it is a bit embarrassing to be reminded of how you sleep with me in light of this rebellion,' he mused and touched an idle finger to her hot cheek. 'All right, you win.'

Her eyes widened and flew to his.

'Unfortunately, it's going to delay Daisy's pony, not to mention her opportunity to prove something to us, but be that as it may.' And he switched the key on, glanced in the mirror and swung the car into a U-turn so they were going back the way they'd come.

'You!' Arizona whispered, going quite pale with rage.

'It's up to you, my dear,' he said grimly.

'Turn around then,' she commanded. 'But while I may do this interview, don't expect me to be anything like putty in your hands for... the rest of my life, probably!'

He laughed softly as he did another U-turn and said, 'Now that is throwing down the gauntlet, Arizona.'

'Well, you didn't even have to look coy.'

Arizona breathed deeply and stopped what she was doing. Which was changing out of her violet suit. The bedroom of the Sydney house was bathed in sunlight. It was a very hot day, and Declan had just come in, closed the door and leant his broad shoulders against it.

'No,' she said turning her back on him to hang her jacket up carefully.

'How about a swim?' he suggested lazily. 'Seeing as we've got that out of the way. Incidentally—' he straightened and strolled over to her '—you were very good, Arizona. Cool, beautiful, poised—definitely an asset.'

'Good. You can send me back to Scawfell now.'

'I thought you'd decided Daisy deserved her chance. But anyway,' he murmured, his blue gaze drifting down her body, 'I have other plans for you at the moment.'

'No,' she whispered through a suddenly dry throat. 'You can't do this to me.'

'What, as a matter of interest, do you think I'm about to do?'

'Something along the putty in your hands line?' She was only able to say it barely audibly but she was able to add, 'You won't enjoy it unless you have a preference for overpowering women.'

'Look, Arizona,' he said abruptly and took her hands. 'I think we can deal better than this. I'm sorry you felt so much against going public, and I'm still not sure what your reasons were, but it was for the best, believe me. You know, you yourself told me only a couple of weeks ago that I was managing our lives very capably.'

'I didn't altogether mean that.' She stopped and bit her lip.

'Tell me what you meant, then.'

She grimaced, but it was too late. 'I suppose I feel— you said just now that I was an asset, that's how I feel. As if I'm a parcel of shares, or something inanimate that you can move around at will. I . . .' She stopped and shrugged.

'On the other hand, didn't we agree that for two people not in love although greatly attracted to each other,' he asked gently, 'you would live your life and I would live mine?'

She couldn't answer, only stare at him.

'And, when you think about it,' he continued with that same deadly gentleness, 'it's only where our lives have collided that I've made arrangements, which I consider are in all our best interests. For the rest of the time, you're free to go your own road. You're free to do what you once told me you liked doing best. You have the means now, moreover, to do it in great style. Or—' he paused and searched her eyes in a manner that made her wish devoutly she could run away and hide from him '—are you trying to tell me that those things you once liked to do best are beginning to pall?'

Yes, she answered, but in her mind. *Because I don't want to spend ninety per cent of my life doing my own thing, because I want to be loved and be able to love you openly. Why can't I just tell you? Is it pride, stupid vaunted pride? Or am I still afraid I'll end up like my mother?*

'Arizona?' He waited with courteous attention for her to speak, but when she didn't, said, 'Or is it a desire to be able to queen it over all and sundry as my wife, and spend my money in a much more public way?'

For a moment, she thought she was going to faint, so great was the hurt. But a moment later, she merely freed her hands and said quietly, 'No. None of those, Declan. I'm quite happy to continue our... purely business affair—with a dash of physical attraction thrown in, let's not forget that.' She managed to smile a queer tense little smile at him. 'And if you don't mind, I think I will go for a swim.'

'You think that will solve this—impasse?'

'I have no idea,' she whispered.

'Then let me make another suggestion.'

She broke then. 'Please,' she said in sudden desperation, 'that's like asking me to prostitute myself in your bed unless—' tears, foolish tears started to slip down her cheeks '—that's what you believe I've been doing all along?'

He stood like a rock for a full minute, watching the way she attempted to stem the flow, how her shoulders shook, his eyes unreadable, his mouth set in a hard line. Then he sighed, put an arm round her shoulders and pulled her against him, which she had not the composure to resist, and said against her hair, 'No, but I think we may be two of a kind. I'm sorry. Would you consider coming to bed with me because I rather desperately need you?'

Three days later, he said to her, 'Do you think we should take pity on Daisy?'

They were in bed, it was very early and raining heavily. Arizona moved her cheek on his chest and smiled faintly. 'You must be a mind-reader. I woke up thinking about her.'

'Then we'll go home this morning. How do you feel?'

'Fine. Don't I look it?' she asked whimsically.

'I can't see that much of you at the moment,' he murmured and drew aside the sheet that covered them. 'That's better.'

'Is that a way to tell how fine a person is—'

'In your case you're looking exceptionally fine, but then, you always do like this.' He moved his hand down her back to her hips.

'I was going to say—'

'However,' he interrupted, 'as you were probably going to say, I also need to look into your eyes and there's one *particularly* fine way to do that. Let me show you.'

'Declan,' she said on a breath, moments later, when he'd sat her up and guided her to sit astride him while he lay back with the pillows heaped up behind him.

'Arizona?' He put his hands under her arms and drew them down the outline of her body from her armpits to the swell of her breasts that lay like pale, pink-tipped orbs to the slenderness of her waist then the curve of her hips and finally, her thighs. 'You were saying?'

'Nothing—of great moment,' she said with an effort. 'Just that I don't believe it's my eyes you're concentrating on, particularly.'

'You're wrong, you know,' he said wryly, stroking the tender skin of her inner thighs. 'I love looking into your eyes when I'm doing something like this. Don't you like it?'

She put her hands on his chest and considered. 'If I could be allowed to—come down to your level, eventually,' she said gravely.

'Be my guest.'

She smiled gently. 'All in good time, Mr. Holmes.' And slipped her fingers through the springy black hair on his chest with concentration, her lashes veiling her eyes.

'Arizona,' he said suddenly and differently.

She looked up and didn't know it but with a tinge of wariness.

'Don't . . . hide from me,' he said, not quite evenly. 'Nor is there anything to be afraid of.'

Isn't there? she wondered but said, 'I'm not.'

'Good. Come here then,' he commanded softly.

'This was your idea,' she murmured with a genuine flicker of humour curving her lips.

'For my sins,' he agreed and cupped her breasts until a tremor ran through her. 'That's better,' he added lazily and with a wicked glint.

'I have to wonder why,' she murmured ruefully as her nipples flowered beneath his fingers and a tide of living desire flowed through her.

'I'd hate to think I was alone in—experiencing this.'

'Well, you're not,' she said on a little jolt of breath but was able to add with composure—but only just— 'I'm coming down, Declan, be warned.'

Then she was in his arms, lying on the length of him, and they were laughing at the same time as they climaxed in a way that was new to them, stunning but with warmth and ... tenderness? she wondered. Of a kind they'd not known before?

Daisy was fine when they got home but thrilled to see them, as were Sarah and Richard, and a mood of excitement gripped the house when the subject of the new pony was brought out into the open.

'Where, er, does one acquire new ponies at very short notice?' Declan asked Arizona rather ruefully.

'Rosemary,' she replied promptly.

He raised a wry eyebrow at her. 'What would we do without Rosemary—but how come?'

'Rosemary is very into horses and president of the local pony club. If anyone can dig up a suitable pony for Daisy, she can. She also gives riding lessons.'

'Then I think we ought to pay a call on Rosemary right now.'

'Well, I'm sure Daisy will understand if we leave it until tomorrow.'

He looked at her steadily for a moment then said quietly, 'I won't be here tomorrow, unfortunately. And I do feel I should keep faith with Daisy, having instigated this, by at least looking over some ponies with her.'

Arizona hid her sudden inner pang by saying with a grin, 'Well, I'm sure Rosemary will be delighted to see you! Do you mind if I stay here and unpack? I would imagine Daisy will feel doubly important and grown-up if you two go alone.'

He looked at her searchingly but said nothing and that's how the rest of the day was organized.

When they got home Daisy was almost speechless with happiness and succumbed finally to a storm of tears brought about by overexcitement.

'Sorry,' Declan said when they were alone at last, after Arizona had finally managed to get Daisy to sleep. 'Here.' He handed her a glass of wine.

Arizona sank into a chair beside the fireplace. 'Thanks! I'm going to enjoy this.'

He sat down opposite and told her about the pony, which was due to arrive in a few days, and passed on Rosemary's good wishes. Then he said slowly, 'I'm sorry about this, but it's another trip to the States. I've—acquired a television station and there's a lot to bone up on.' He smiled briefly. 'Pay television, cable television and the like.'

Her eyes widened. 'That sounds like ... really big time.'

'Hopefully.'

'How long?'

'Three weeks.' He gestured. 'Maybe a bit longer, but I'll definitely be home for Christmas.'

'Christmas,' she murmured. 'That's not that far away now, I'll have to start making plans.'

'You don't mind?'

Arizona looked across at him and said honestly, 'Yes, of course, but I'll have plenty to occupy me.'

'Good girl,' he said almost absently.

Arizona sipped her wine and laid her head back, mainly, she thought, so that he couldn't see her eyes.

It surprised her, therefore, when he came, gently prised the glass from her fingers and pulled her to her feet, and said, 'It's going to be a hell of a long three weeks.'

She trembled suddenly and he felt it through his hands and frowned. He said, 'What is it?'

'Nothing,' she said huskily. 'I think I'm a bit like Daisy. Just in need of a good night's sleep.'

He paused, watched her narrowly, then dropped a light kiss on her hair. He also said gravely, 'I would offer to come with you but I have an incredibly early start so I'm flying back to town this evening.'

'Now?'

'In about half an hour. Think you can keep your eyes open long enough to wave me off?'

She did, and went inside, hugging herself, and went straight to bed. It was not such a simple matter to get to sleep, however, although she kept telling herself to hold onto those minutes of warmth and tenderness that had happened only that morning, and to use them to combat not only the loneliness but the lack of understanding as to why she couldn't be told of his plans sometimes, why she always had to find out at the last minute... Why?

*   *   *

In fact he came home early from his trip, only two and a half weeks after he'd left, and he drove down, so she didn't even have the whir and roar of the helicopter to forewarn her. She was also in her beloved rose garden, on her knees, digging and watering with her hands dirty, a streak of mud on her chin, wearing her old dungarees when she heard a car and decided to ignore it, until she heard Daisy.

'Declan, Declan—you're home!' Daisy called joyfully. 'I've called my pony Pippa and I can nearly sit on her on my own!'

Arizona stilled, her eyes widening.

'Well, you are a clever girl!' Declan's deep tones came quite clearly round the corner of the house. 'Where is everyone?'

'Sarah and Richard are playing with friends, Ben is staying with one of his new school friends and Cloris is cooking. It's Christmas soon, did you know? And we're all on holiday!'

'Indeed, I do. What about Arizona?'

'I don't know where she is. In the garden prob'ly. She does a lot of gardening because she's cross.'

Arizona froze in the act of getting up off her knees.

'Cross?' Declan's voice expressed quizzical surprise.

'Yes,' Daisy confided.

'Why is she cross, do you think?'

'I don't know but she *is*,' Daisy insisted. 'Maybe it's because you're not here,' she added ingenuously.

Arizona groaned quite silently, got up swiftly and took flight. It did her little good, because he found her not five minutes later in the toolshed.

'Declan!' she said without having to simulate surprise as she turned and discovered him leaning against the doorway, and dropped a trowel.

'Arizona,' he answered amusedly. 'Sorry, I didn't mean to give you a fright.'

'But—it's not three weeks yet,' she protested, totally foolishly, she knew.

'Well, I'm sorry about that, too—would you like me to go away for another half week?'

'No. I mean, no. I...was surprised, that's all. Welcome home!'

'Thanks,' he said but didn't move. 'What's this I hear about you being cross?' he added, his blue gaze quite grave now, but it didn't fool her for a moment. She knew he was laughing at her.

'Cross?' She raised an eyebrow. 'I don't know what you mean.'

'I have it on the best authority.'

Arizona closed her eyes and wished fervently that she didn't blush so easily because she could feel the heat pouring into her cheeks and knew it was useless to dissemble any further. She could also think of absolutely nothing to say.

He straightened. 'So were you?'

'No,' she said a little bleakly. 'Well, if so I didn't realize—and Daisy could be exaggerating.'

He laughed softly. 'You heard?'

'I heard,' she agreed.

'And ran away?' he suggested.

'And ran away.'

'Do you think she's right about the cause of it?'

Arizona sighed, examined her dirty hands then looked into his eyes. 'Possibly.'

'That's very gratifying,' he murmured.

'I'm sure it is,' Arizona returned a shade tartly.

'Because I have to tell you,' he continued, 'that I have been singularly, er, cross over these past two and a half weeks, as well. What do you think that means?'

The corners of her mouth started to twitch. 'You . . . missed my home cooking?'

They laughed together then he said, 'Come here.'

'I'm filthy.'

'I don't mind in the slightest.'

She came. And a little later she indicated she'd like to be released, which he did immediately, but it was only so she could wind her arms round his neck with a queer little sigh.

'Better?' he said gently.

'Much better,' she whispered. But it was only a couple of days later that they had a row, the contents of which she found unbelievable . . .

It started after breakfast when he said casually, 'Arizona, I think you should invite your mother down for Christmas.'

'What?' She blinked at him and stopped what she was doing, which was wrapping Christmas presents on the floor in her study with the door firmly closed against any spying children. Then she said flatly, 'No, I don't think I should, but why?'

'Why not?' he said with some irony.

'Look, I don't understand,' she persisted.

'You said yourself a little while ago that it was about time you stopped feuding with her.'

'I know but—have you stopped feuding with your father?' she asked with a frown.

'No, but there is no mystery about my father.'

Arizona sat back on her heels. 'What do you mean?'

'Put simply—' he paused '—I'd like to meet your mother. But for some reason or another, it would appear as if you're hiding her from me.'

Arizona gasped. 'I . . . hesitate to repeat myself but what do you mean, Declan?'

'That she is not to be found, Arizona. Want to tell me why?'

'Not to be found,' Arizona repeated and then, as full implication of this hit her, 'have you . . . been looking for her?'

He said quite simply and coolly, 'Yes.'

She swallowed. 'How dare you, Declan Holmes. How—I don't believe this—'

'Well, before you get too dramatic, Arizona, is there any reason I *shouldn't* meet your mother? Such as her being a criminal or a—' But he stopped as Arizona picked up a box of games that were to be a Christmas present for Richard, and flung it at him.

The result of this was that the box missed him as he dodged, but they were showered with dice, little chessmen, ludo markers and the like.

'You're unbelievably childish at times, Arizona,' he said grimly and hauled her to her feet unceremoniously.

'No, I'm *not*,' she said, panting. '*You* are unbelievably underhand and conniving, you have no right—and all the money in the world, all the television stations in the world don't give you the right to hound my mother or me like this and—'

'On the contrary, I have every right to protect what is mine.'

She stared at him disbelievingly and with an almost paralysing sense of shock. 'Do you seriously believe that, Declan? That my mother and I have concocted a devious plan to milk you dry? Well, you're right, of course,' she heard herself say. 'I'm only sorry I didn't get you in for a bit longer, but all the same, I'm still your wife and it's going to cost you an awful lot of money to—get rid of me.'

'There's only one problem with that, Arizona,' he said roughly. 'I have no intention of getting rid of you.'

CHAPTER NINE

THE silence was electric. Until she broke it.

'You can't keep me against my will, Declan.'

'Try me, Arizona,' he said grimly.

'That's ridiculous. Do you plan to lock me up?'

'Oh, I don't think I'll have to go that far, not before Christmas, at least—would you run out on the kids now? That *would* be utterly conclusive, wouldn't it?'

'Damn you,' she said angrily.

'And once you've had time for some sober reflection,' he drawled, 'you may see things my way, after all. I'm going up to town now. I'll be back on Christmas Eve. Don't do anything rash, Arizona, will you?'

But although he waited with polite insolence, she was speechless with rage, and he left her, closing the door gently behind him.

'When is Declan coming back?' Daisy said fretfully a few days later. They were decorating the Christmas tree.

'When it suits him,' Sarah said pertly. 'You can't pin a man like Declan down, Daisy.'

'Sarah,' Arizona said, frowning, 'that's an ... odd thing to say.'

'She heard it said,' Richard contributed. 'Didn't you, Sarah?'

Sarah threw a tinsel bauble at him. 'Don't tell!' she commanded.

'Why not? You said it,' Richard reasoned, and threw the bauble back, whereupon Sarah reached for some tiny bells.

'Stop it,' Arizona warned. 'And I think you better tell me what you heard said, Sarah.'

Sarah sighed theatrically, glared at her twin then shrugged. 'It's what Maddy Mason's mum said, that's all.'

'When did she say this?' Arizona went on hanging things on the tree and contrived to keep her voice calm, although not to be brooked.

'When I went to play with Maddy the other day. She's very nosy, Mrs. Mason. She was asking me all sorts of questions about you and Declan, she had that magazine, too.'

'What kind of questions?'

'How much time he spends here at Scawfell, how much time you spend with him. It was when I said not a lot that she said he's a hard man to pin down and it might not be a real marriage anyway, she was sort of talking to herself then but I—'

'Sarah, I don't think you should discuss those kind of things with other people,' Arizona broke in.

'If you'd let me finish,' Sarah said with ten-year-old hauteur, '*that* was when I told her it was really none of her business. I don't think I'll be invited to play with Maddy Mason again,' she added with a giggle. 'But it's true, you don't spend a lot of time together, do you, Arizona? I mean, it's not really like having a mother and father again. Not that it bothers us,' she added with the absolute honesty that reinforced Arizona's opinion that Sarah was going to be one of those uncomfortable people who always called a spade a spade, 'but there's always our baby,' she finished and rolled her eyes in Daisy's direction.

'If you're calling me a baby, Sarah,' Daisy said hotly, 'I am not! Declan himself told me I was very grown-up. That's why I want to *show* him how well I can ride now,' she added, but with a distinct break in her voice.

'See what I mean?' Sarah said out of the corner of her mouth with a worldly little sigh. But she went on, 'Listen, Daisy, Ben will be home tomorrow, you can show him!'

Daisy brightened and they finished the tree amicably.

It was Cloris who completed another difficult day for Arizona by saying to her after the children were in bed, 'You don't look well, pet. I'm tempted to call Mr. Holmes and let him know you need a break.'

'Cloris.' Arizona swallowed irritation, disbelief and horror. 'Don't. I'm fine.'

'Well, he did say to me once if I thought you needed anything just to let him know.'

Arizona blinked at her. '*When?*'

'I can't remember exactly,' Cloris said airily and added, 'you know, I'm sure he'd be here if he could.'

'He'll be here on Christmas Eve, Cloris,' Arizona said and bit her lip in case any of her prejudice on the subject had shown through.

'Oh, well, that's less than a week away now, and then I'm sure we'll all be happy and more comfortable.'

All Arizona could do was walk out, as normally as possible, she hoped, but instead of taking herself to bed she went for a walk down to the cliff edge and sat on the turf with her knees drawn up, her chin resting on them—and the leaden heart within her breast feeling even worse than usual as she contemplated the fact that she couldn't go on much longer under this intolerable strain, could no longer reconcile sleeping with a man who believed the things Declan Holmes believed of her. And contemplated the bitter sense of failure in her heart, because although she had slept with him and laughed with him and thought there was a new, unique and growing sense of tenderness between them, she couldn't have been more wrong. Nothing had changed his doubts of her, apparently, nothing.

But what to do about the children? she mused painfully. *In the long run is it going to help them to have me as tormented as I am? Did Sarah not demonstrate today that the imperfections of our marriage are becoming obvious to all and sundry? Has Daisy not flowered under his care as much as mine?*

She shivered suddenly, dropped her face into her hands and came to a decision. And the next morning saw her driving away from Scawfell on the pretext of a last-minute Christmas shopping spree, having mentioned the possibility that she might spend the night in Sydney with Declan, having reassured Daisy that Ben would be home today, and having left with a heart almost breaking because she had no idea whether she would return.

She made one call in the village, which took her about half an hour, and then about ten miles south of Sydney she pulled into a garage to fill up with petrol and got the surprise of her life when her new gardener peered in through the offside window, cleared his throat and said, 'Sorry about this, Mrs. Holmes, but Declan asked me to, well, let him know if you made any surprise moves.'

'*What?*'

'*Are* you going to see him, Mrs. Holmes? If so, there's no problem but—'

A red mist of rage swam before Arizona's eyes but she pulled herself out of it with a Herculean effort and said sweetly, 'But if not you'd like to know where I'm going? Look, why don't I save you a lot of trouble? Where's your car?'

'Uh—over there.' He pointed and Arizona recognized the car parked neatly off the driveway, could not imagine how she'd missed that it was following her but didn't care either.

'Is it locked?'

'Well, yes—'

'Good, then hop in.'

'Mrs. Holmes—'

'Do as I say,' Arizona commanded with such a blaze of anger in her grey eyes that the ex-naval man cum gardener did just that, although not precisely happily.

'Where are we going?' he asked tentatively as Arizona paid for her petrol and drove off.

'You'll see.' And she spoke not another word to him as she drove fast and furiously right into the heart of Sydney Town, parked illegally at the base of a tall building and commanded him to accompany her inside.

The foyer of the building was extremely impressive, and she had to pause for a moment to study the direction board, but she soon saw what she was looking for and with an imperious wave of her hand dictated to the poor man to follow her. They got out on the twentieth floor, and she swept into the reception office she sought, didn't even blink at its magnificence nor at three men all conservatively dressed and apparently standing in conference as she approached the desk.

Where she said in clear, crisp tones, 'I'm Mrs. Declan Holmes and I would like to see my husband *immediately*.'

You could have heard a pin drop for about half a minute before the clearly flustered receptionist said, 'I . . . I'm afraid he's in a meeting, Mrs. Holmes, but his secretary—'

'Then you better get him out of the meeting, unless he wishes to be confronted by an extremely angry wife in front of whoever he's meeting with!'

'Yes, Mrs. Holmes,' the poor young woman whispered and grabbed a phone while the three men blinked and gaped, and the gardener looked as if he wished the floor would open up and swallow him.

A minute later Declan strolled into the reception area looking dark, inscrutable but curiously relaxed, unless you happened to know that glint of steel in his eyes. And he drawled, 'Ah, Arizona. Come to see me, I believe. Will you come through?'

'No, I will not, nor did I come to see *you* particularly, Declan, merely to drop your watchdog off! In fact you're the last person I'm desirous of seeing at

the moment, although since I'm here I might as well
tell you how utterly contemptible I find you—'

'And that's enough, my dear,' he murmured, and
closing on her, took her elbow in a vice-like grip and
forced her to walk beside him out into the corridor.
Nor did he relax his grip as he summoned a lift and
they rode down to the basement garage swiftly and
silently, with Arizona, now that the magnificence of
her rage had spent itself although not the cold outward
manifestation of it, inwardly shaking a little.

'Get in,' he said as they came up to the Saab.

'No.'

'Don't make me have to force you, Arizona,' he
recommended through his teeth.

She looked around but there was not a soul in sight,
and got in.

He drove her to the Point Piper house, which gave
her a little time to collect her nerves, and she got out
proudly and walked inside in front of him, her head
held high while she murmured a formal greeting to
the housekeeper who opened the door. But when she
turned to go into what she knew was his study, he
took her elbow again and directed her upstairs to the
master bedroom. And although he shoved his hands
in his trouser pockets after he'd closed the door firmly,
there was menace in every line of his tall figure and
something so cold in his eyes, she shivered
involuntarily.

'Well?' he said but only after subjecting her to the
coolest, most insolent stripping her of her clothes with
his eyes imaginable, so that she looked at her stylish,
sleeveless, camellia pink linen dress with its slim lines

and long skirt as if to assure herself it was still there—
and then clench her hands into fists.

'Don't ever have me followed again, Declan,' she
said clearly, her anger refuelling itself, 'in case I'm
tempted to embarrass you even more. And while we're
on the subject, I might as well tell you, we're finished,
you and I, nor is there *any* way you can stop me
leaving you, and don't even mention the children because I have it on good authority this time that they're
well aware our marriage is a sham and I can only see
it hurting them now if I stay to fight on. But let me
tell you, perhaps most importantly, since I know how
you doubt me on these matters, that I went to see a
solicitor this morning and I signed a waiver to all your
worldly goods, or even half of them.' And she stripped
her shoulder purse off, opened it to extract a document
from it, which she dropped on the floor between them.
'I want nothing from you, Declan,' she added proudly.
'Not a single thing. Nor does my mother, because,
since she's a nun in a closed order these days, you
see, there's not a lot she could do with a single cent.'

But if she'd hoped to shock him, he merely narrowed his eyes and didn't even glance at the paper on
the floor. And he said, 'Why did you wait to leave
me to tell me all this, Arizona?'

She took a breath, turned away abruptly and strode
over to the French window overlooking the pool, to
see with some surprise that the day had clouded over
heavily and that there was lightning in the sky. Then
she said in a suddenly toneless, weary voice, 'You
married me, not my mother. Anyway, I did tell you
about her. Why didn't you believe me, Declan?'

The room was very quiet, apart from the rumble of thunder in the distance. Until he said, 'Arizona, have you any idea what simply the sheen of your hair, the curve of your cheek, the line of your lips have done to me over the past nearly three years?'

She turned slowly, as if she couldn't believe what she was hearing, and her lips parted. Then she shook her head, dazed, as if to say, *No, this can't be for real—*

And he hadn't moved from the door and it seemed to her as if there was an acre of pewter blue velvet carpet between them. 'I...' She licked her lips. 'I don't know what you mean. You don't trust me, you—'

'Do you trust me?' he broke in. 'But no, I haven't been able to trust—or rather believe that you love me. For one thing, you've never told me, never reversed those views you told me you held of yourself nor told me I might have restored your faith in men—or even just one man. To this day,' he said very quietly, 'I have no idea whether I mean more to you than Pete, who you married for the sake of convenience.'

To her horror, Arizona discovered that her legs were no longer steady and she sank to the carpet on her knees then sat back on her heels. 'But I showed you, I *must* have shown you that,' she said hoarsely.

'Did you?'

She had to tilt her head back as he towered over her for a moment then sat down on the end of the bed beside her.

'Did you sleep with him the way you sleep with me, for instance?' he went on. 'I have no way of knowing how to differentiate.'

'You do—you know I'd never—that it had never happened that way for me before... Didn't that tell you... anything?'

He shrugged slightly. 'It gave me hope at times. And there were times when you indicated you weren't happy with the way things were, but on every last opportunity I presented you with to tell me why, you— slipped away from me.'

'And it means so much to you?' she whispered, shaken suddenly to her core.

'It means,' he said quietly, 'that until you tell me these things, I can't know whether you love me.'

'And it's never occurred to you,' she said barely, 'that I might have the same problem?'

'Such as?'

'Declan,' she whispered, 'I have no way of knowing whether you love me. In fact I have a lot of evidence to the contrary. You're hardly ever with me, you... force me to do everything your way, you use the kids to hold me—'

'Did you never stop to wonder why?'

'Because you mistrust me,' she said distraughtly. 'Because you can't ever forget Pete—'

'Only you can do that for me, Arizona.'

Their eyes locked then he added, 'If it means anything to you, the fact that I will never let you go, if it means anything that possibly the worst year of my life was the year you were married to Pete, but it has to be closely followed by these months when I've waited to hear you say just three words, or at least explain better why you couldn't. If it means *anything* that the reason I've stayed away from you as much as I have was that I was seeking a form of protection against falling more and more in love with you, if that was possible.'

Arizona stared at him with stunned eyes. Then she said uncertainly, as if she couldn't trust her voice, 'Can I . . . can I start at the beginning?'

He nodded.

It took her a few minutes to compose her thoughts, and she plucked at the carpet before lifting her eyes to his. 'I've told you about my mother already, or most of it, but it was only when she began to see, in my late teens, how much I despised her for the way she was that *she*, I suppose, stopped and tried to take stock. It was too late for me, though, I—' she paused and sighed '—rejected her. By that time I'd left school and was living on campus at teacher's college. She hung on for a year or so, trying to make a home for me that I didn't want, trying to show me that she'd not reformed so much but was a different person now, but I didn't believe it, and then one day she came and told me that she was going into this convent. I . . . I'm afraid I laughed. I can only say in my defence that I'd never known my father, that I'd been to twelve schools in every state of the country and I'd lived through four . . . men, none of them bad men particularly, none of them who didn't try at times to treat me like a daughter, but all the same, *all* of them walking out on her. I . . . now know I can never forgive myself for laughing at her, for not trying to support her because she is my mother, and she went into every last one of those relationships believing this was *it*. Even believing, I think, that it would create a better life for me.'

'Go on,' Declan said gently after a long pause.

'But the truth of the matter was that I felt betrayed even though I'd done all that rejecting. Strange, isn't it?'

'Not in the circumstances, and if you were only nineteen or so,' he said quietly.

Arizona shrugged. 'I also, at nineteen, wondered if I might have fallen in love with a fellow student. He, well, at times he used to make my heart go bang and make me feel quite breathless and weak at the knees.' She grimaced. 'But, although everyone else seeemd to be experimenting with sex, I began to dislike the proprietorial way he started to treat me and I couldn't be persuaded to go to bed with him, probably because I had my mother at the back of my mind all the time, and it turned into a rather unpleasant fiasco.'

'He got nasty?' Declan suggested.

'He—' Arizona paused and sighed. 'I gained a reputation for being—well, there were two versions, a tease or frigid.'

Declan smiled slightly and said, 'We men have very fragile egos, I'm afraid. But if nothing else, didn't that convince you you weren't about to follow in your mother's footsteps?'

It was Arizona's turn to smile, unamused. 'Yes although I came to doubt that later,' she said barely audibly. 'Uh...what it did leave me with was the feeling that I might have inherited her...poor judgment, but there was something else, I began to sympathise with her then, in a mostly subconscious way, but I did think, well, I convinced myself I'd be better leaving the whole tribe of men alone. It just...wasn't that easy, though,' she said with a sigh.

'Not with your looks and your figure, I imagine it wasn't.'

She looked at him suddenly. 'The funny thing was the more I froze them off the more...' She stopped and bit her lip.

'That's something you don't have to tell me about, Arizona,' he said, not without irony.

'Anyway,' she continued after a moment, 'then I got the job at Scawfell. And it was a revelation,' she said with a little, oddly helpless gesture.

'Tell me why.'

'I fell in love with the house, with the country, with the kids. I felt for the first time as if I had a *place* in, well, in the scheme of things. I discovered talents I didn't know I possessed. I was needed, really needed—and I knew by then that my mother only needed God. I went up to see her once, you see, and she was a different person, serene, confident, loving yes, but...' She shrugged. 'So that's how it was, Declan.' She studied her hands then looked into his eyes to see if he understood.

'My dear, I think I've always understood that,' he said and reached out a hand. She put hers into it after a moment. 'One only had to see you with the kids, to see that. So, tell me about Pete now.'

She swallowed. 'Pete...put a proposition to me after I'd been there for nearly a year. He told me he'd fallen in love with me but he knew I didn't reciprocate. He told me, no, he asked me to tell him a little of why I was the way I was and I did. He then...Declan...' She stopped.

'Go on.' The pressure of his hand on hers increased, but as if to give her courage.

'He told me he had a disability, quite a complicated rare condition.' She paused. 'One . . . of the side effects of it was that he was impotent, and he told me that apart from losing his wife, it was the most shattering thing that had ever happened to him. That it had knocked his self-esteem about to the extent that it had seriously affected his creativity. It amazed and horrified him, he said, to discover that although it was a side effect of his condition, that although no-one need know other than himself and his doctor, yet he was getting around like half a man and couldn't help living his life as if it was written all over him. And so, he said, while he couldn't consummate a marriage, if I needed a home and security, if I needed some respite from my own problems, it was possible that we could help each other out. That it would be a way for him no longer to feel as if everyone could guess that he had this awful problem, a way for him to get back to work, he hoped.'

'And you believed that?' Declan said after a long silence.

She glanced at him but couldn't tell much from his expression. 'I had lots of doubts,' she confessed. 'But I had seen him all but tearing his hair out trying to get the genius that had made him such a wonderful architect flowing. He was, by then, a friend I trusted and a confidante and we were—comfortable with each other. On the other hand, I couldn't help wondering what would happen if he got better and I said that to him. *He* said it would always be up to me. So I looked at the options, which seemed to me to be pretty bleak, and I took the plunge.' She stopped and swallowed.

'Did he ever get better, Arizona?'

'No,' she whispered. 'At least, I don't think so. Because he never tried to sleep with me, he never even brought the subject up in the year we were married. But if I did do one thing for him, if I was ever able to repay him for all that I gained, it was to see him working again with all his old flair and to know that I must have been able to alter his perception of his self-esteem as seen through the eyes of others. Nor would I ever have told a soul this, Declan, I would have kept faith with him, for everything he did for me, for ever, if it hadn't been for you.'

'My dear,' Declan said, in curiously strained voice, 'forgive me.' And then he stood up and pulled her to her feet and was cupping her face gently, kissing the tears that had at last started to flow. 'There's only one thing I need to know now,' he said at last. 'If *I've* been able to alter your perception of yourself, the one that told you you couldn't fall in love, and never with me.'

'Oh, that.' The tears fell faster and she kissed the inside of his wrist and tasted them salty on her lips. 'If only you knew how many times I wanted to say it, or knew how lonely and miserable I've felt without you, and wondered and tormented myself with the thought that the rest of our lives were going to be like this, and tortured myself wondering if I did tell you, whether I'd be like my mother, so...somehow *vulnerable* so as to invite desertion and all the rest, but if it means anything to you, Declan, I love you so much that every time you leave me, every time I wake up without you beside me from the very first time we made love, *all* the time I haven't known how you felt, I've died and die a little inside. Sorry...'

'Don't,' he said harshly and held her in his arms so that she could barely breathe. 'Don't apologize for loving me. I should be the one—'

'No,' she said softly. 'Perhaps we should concentrate on how much we love each other?'

'Where were you going today?' he said later.

They were still clothed but lying on the bed in each other's arms.

'Oh!' Arizona started guiltily as memories of the earlier part of the day came back to her. 'Oh, no. I feel terrible.'

'Why?' he asked quizzically and kissed her hair.

'I...the things I did. And said, in front of heaven knows who, but your receptionist for one, and the gardener. I feel *really* terrible now. On top of which—' she sat up with real perturbation '—my car has probably been clamped or towed away—'

'Come back here,' Declan interposed with a laugh in his voice and took her in his arms again. 'You were magnificent,' he added.

'I was awful— Do you mean that? How—'

He put a finger to her lips. 'My dear Arizona, don't you know that that's why I love you so much? For your total refusal ever to be intimidated by me. For fighting me every inch of the way—'

'That's not quite true.'

'Yes, it is. But also for—' he paused and threaded his fingers through hers '—making love to me like no other, with a mixture of joy, honesty and rapture, making me aware of your likes and dislikes at times,' he said gravely.

'I haven't done much of that.'

'You have. You definitely ticked me off for treating you like an object once,' he reminded her.

'Well, was I wrong, though?'

'No,' he conceded. 'What you may not have realized at the time was that I was nearly at the end of my tether. Because I'd almost convinced myself you'd come up from the beach that day after looking so lonely and somehow lost, and beg me not to leave you again because you couldn't live without me.'

Arizona caught her breath. 'I...I'm doing that now, Declan,' she said unsteadily. 'I mean, I know you'll have to go away from time to time but—'

'Don't cry,' he said into her hair. 'You won't be able to prise me away with a crowbar now—'

'But I'm trying to tell you I do understand that there will have to be times—'

'Times, yes, but the absolute minimum now, my darling. You still haven't told me, though. Where you were going today?'

'Oh, that. I *was* coming to see you. I was going to try to tell you all this and then, if I couldn't sort of prove it to you, I was also going to go...away, but I hadn't worked out where, other than to see my mother first. That's how I knew where to come,' she added. 'I had your card in my purse—do you remember giving it to me?'

'Only too well, unfortunately. Arizona...' He stopped, sighed and said simply, 'Thank God.'

'For coming to your office? And creating all that mayhem—your poor ex-naval friend must be...I don't know.'

'Wondering what he's done to deserve being treated like a loose cannon between us?' he supplied with a crooked little grin.

'Yes.' She smiled ruefully.

'I love you,' he said, his grin fading.

'Would you like to know what I love about you?' she answered huskily.

'Yes . . .'

She told him, and presently he helped her out of her dress and made love to her in a way that caused her to give thanks rather fervently.

'Tell me,' he said gently.

'I wondered once, not so long ago,' she said, 'whether there was something new between us, something incredibly lovely and tender that—made me want to die for you. Then I thought I must have imagined it.'

'And now?'

'Now I know I didn't imagine it.'

He kissed her and held her very close. And later he said, 'Would it be possible for us both to go and see your mother?'

'Yes, I think so.' Arizona sighed with pure happiness.

A year later, Christmas Day dawned bright and clear at Scawfell and began with a squabble. 'It's *my* turn to give him his bath,' Daisy said. 'I'm nearly seven and a half now, and I know all about babies, so you can just go away, Sarah!'

'Daisy, darling—'

'Well, it's true, isn't it, Arizona?' Daisy turned to her heatedly. 'You've shown me how, and anyway, I'm not the baby any longer, am I? He is.'

'Oh, definitely. Why don't you bath him and let Sarah dress him?'

'And I'm taking him for a walk in his pram,' Richard contributed. 'It's his first Christmas, after all, and we are both boys. There'll probably be lots of times when he'll need to get away from you two, not to mention Cloris!' he added to his sisters.

'Well, I'll have to be content with taking his picture,' Ben said wryly, looking interestedly at the new camera he'd just received. 'I know—I'll make a pictorial record of how baby mania has overtaken this family!'

'Baby mania?' Declan said some time later when he'd firmly closed the door of the green suite so that Arizona could rest before they embarked on the rigours of Christmas dinner. 'How long is this going to last, do you think?'

Arizona glanced down at her son, who was barely six weeks old but was appearing to thrive on all the attention. 'I don't know, but we do truly feel like a family now, and they're really very sweet, aren't they? But there's something I wanted to tell you, Declan.'

'Oh?' He sat down on the bed beside her and also glanced at his sleeping son in the crib beside the bed. 'That sounds a bit ominous. Have I done something to displease you, Mrs. Holmes? I must say it's quite a while since you cast me that autocratic, do-your-damnedest-Declan, pure grey gaze.'

'I didn't!' Arizona protested laughingly.

'Do you know something, I think, on the odd occasion, you always will.' A wicked little glint lit his eyes.

'This is not one of those—extremely rare occasions,' Arizona said, trying not to smile.

'Ah. What is it then?'

'Well, it's to do with my Christmas present. Not the one that was under the tree this morning,' she said as he raised an eyebrow, and she blushed faintly.

He started to frown. 'You have another one? I—'

'Yes, yes, I do. It's time to—well, it would be all right now to resume—I don't know why this should be so difficult,' she said with sudden exasperation.

'Resume relations do you mean?'

'Yes, which I thought might make rather a nice, if not to say, special sort of present and—'

'I agree, wholeheartedly,' he said gravely.

'But I did also want to,' Arizona went on determinedly, 'say thank you for your patience and the way you were when I was…anyway, thanks,' she said huskily and blinked suspiciously. 'You've been great.'

'Arizona.' He took her hand and with his other hand cupped her cheek. 'You do know why, if that's so, don't you? I thought I might have convinced you that you're not only my wife but the partner of my thoughts, and that anything to do with your welfare is my top priority.'

'Partner of your thoughts,' she said softly. 'That's lovely. Thanks again.'

'These—relations you were talking about,' he said a few minutes later. 'Would it be too decadent to resume them at eleven o'clock in the morning? It looks as if this young man is having an excellent sleep and could be returned to his nursery with impunity.'

'Decadent?' Arizona returned. 'If so, deliciously so, Declan.' And some minutes later, she settled into his arms with a sigh of pure pleasure, but not only that, almost overwhelming love that she now knew was returned in full measure.

Coming Next Month

HARLEQUIN PRESENTS®

THE BEST HAS JUST GOTTEN BETTER!

#1929 A MARRIAGE TO REMEMBER Carole Mortimer
Three years ago Adam Carmichael had walked out on Maggi—
now he was back! Divorce seemed the only way to get him
out of her life for good. But Adam wasn't going to let her go
without a fight!

#1930 RED-HOT AND RECKLESS Miranda Lee
(Scandals!)
Ben Sinclair just couldn't put his schoolboy obsession with
Amber behind him. He *still* thought she could have anything
because she was rich and beautiful. But now Ben had a
chance to get even with her at last....

#1931 TIGER, TIGER Robyn Donald
Leo Dacre was determined to find out what had happened to
his runaway half brother, but Tansy was just as determined
not to tell him! It was a clash of equals...so who would be the
winner?

#1932 FLETCHER'S BABY Anne McAllister
Sam Fletcher never ran away from difficult situations, so
when Josie revealed that she was expecting his child,
marriage seemed the practical solution. And he wasn't going
to take no for an answer!

#1933 THE SECRET MOTHER Lee Wilkinson
(Nanny Wanted!)
Caroline had promised herself that one day she would be
back for Caitlin. Now, four years later, she's applying for the
job of her nanny. Matthew Carran, the interviewer, doesn't
seem to recognize her. But he has a hidden agenda....

#1934 HUSBAND BY CONTRACT Helen Brooks
(Husbands and Wives)
For Donato Vittoria, marriage was a lifetime commitment.
Or so Grace had thought—until she'd discovered his betrayal,
and fled. But in Donato's eyes he was still her husband, and
he wanted her back in his life—and in his bed!

Take 4 bestselling love stories FREE

Plus get a FREE surprise gift!

Free Gift Offer

With a Free Gift proof-of-purchase
from any Harlequin® book, you can receive
a beautiful cubic zirconia pendant.

This stunning marquise-shaped stone is a genuine cubic
zirconia—accented by an 18" gold tone necklace.
(Approximate retail value $19.95)

Send for yours today...
compliments of ◈HARLEQUIN®

To receive your free gift, a cubic zirconia pendant, send us one original proof-of-purchase, photocopies not accepted, from the back of any Harlequin Romance®, Harlequin Presents®, Harlequin Temptation®, Harlequin Superromance®, Harlequin Intrigue®, Harlequin American Romance®, or Harlequin Historicals® title available at your favorite retail outlet, together with the Free Gift Certificate, plus a check or money order for $1.65 U.S./$2.15 CAN. (do not send cash) to cover postage and handling, payable to Harlequin Free Gift Offer. We will send you the specified gift. Allow 6 to 8 weeks for delivery. Offer good until December 31, 1997, or while quantities last. Offer valid in the U.S. and Canada only.

Free Gift Certificate

Name: _____

Address: _____

City: _____ State/Province: _____ Zip/Postal Code: _____

Mail this certificate, one proof-of-purchase and a check or money order for postage and handling to: HARLEQUIN FREE GIFT OFFER 1997. In the U.S.: 3010 Walden Avenue, P.O. Box 9071, Buffalo NY 14269-9057. In Canada: P.O. Box 604, Fort Erie, Ontario L2Z 5X3.

FREE GIFT OFFER   084-KEZ

ONE PROOF-OF-PURCHASE
To collect your fabulous FREE GIFT, a cubic zirconia pendant, you must include this
original proof-of-purchase for each gift with the properly completed Free Gift Certificate.

084-KEZR

Harlequin Romance®
and Harlequin Presents®

bring you two great new miniseries with one thing in common—MEN! They're sexy, successful and available!

You won't want to miss these exciting romances
by some of your favorite authors,
written from the male point of view.

Harlequin Romance® brings you

Starting in January 1998 with Rebecca Winters,
we'll be bringing you one **Bachelor Territory** book
every other month. Look for books by Val Daniels,
Emma Richmond, Lucy Gordon, Heather Allison
and Barbara McMahon.

Harlequin Presents® launches **MAN TALK**
in April 1998 with bestselling author Charlotte Lamb.
Watch for books by Alison Kelly, Sandra Field and
Emma Darcy in June, August and October 1998.

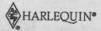 HARLEQUIN®   *There are two sides to every story...
and now it's his turn!*